Alwa

Forever.

PS. BLACK
Romance Author

Edits: Dee's Notes: Proofreading and Editing Services

Cover Design: Coffin Print Designs

Formatting : PS. Black and KB. Row

Proofreader: Toni McPherson

ISBN: 978-1-916536-00-5

Where words fail, music speaks.

-Hans Christian Andersen

Playlist

"I Guess I'm in Love" By Clinton Kane
"Unconditional (Acoustic)" By Sinead Harnett
"All My Life" By K-Ci & JoJo
"Forever and Ever and Always" By Ryan Mack
"Falling Like The Stars" By James Arthur
"Get You The Moon (Feat. Snow)" By Kina, Snow
"Always Remember Us This Way" By Lauren Spencer Smith
"Like I'm Gonna Lose You" By Jasmin Thompson
"Don't Forget About Me" by Cloves
"Broken" By Digga
"Missing You" By 1st Lady
"Lost Without You" by Freya Ridings
"There You'll Be" by Faith Hill
"Ghost" By Justin Bieber
"In The Stars" By Benson Boone
"Dancing In The Sky" By Dani and Lizzy
"Pain's My Only Home" By Zevia
"I'll Never Love Again – Extended Version" By Lady Gaga
"Fix You – Live" by Sam Smith
"Healing Hurts" By BlU Eyes

Always. Forever. is a romance, but there are sad scenes that some readers may struggle to read. Please also note there is mature content.

"You were unsure which pain is worse - the shock of what happened or the ache for what never will."
-Simon Van Booy

Dedication

To my Mum - I wish you could be here
to see this.
I love and miss you so much.

Prologue

Rylee - 20 years old

No more hibernating. With officially finishing my degree to become an accountant, I can say goodbye to late-night-study sessions. It's time to get into the big world and find a job that makes those years that turned me into a hermit worth it. That's tomorrow, though, tonight, I'm out with the girls for a long overdue, well-needed girls' night.

"You never know, you might get some dick tonight. God knows you need it. I'm sure you're a born-again virgin."

"*Toni*," I hiss. I look to the rearview mirror to see if the taxi driver heard my best friend. *Thankfully*, he is watching the road and not us. He's not smirking either, so I'm hoping he didn't—or he is just used to hearing worse. Working for the Baltimore taxi service, I imagine he's heard crazy things from peoples' mouths.

Toni has no filter, especially when she's been drinking. I'm not a prude by any means, but I'm not drunk enough to be talking about how bad I need dick, out loud.

"What? It's true, Ry, we need to get you some meat, ASAP."

I roll my eyes and gaze out the window. The nightlife of Baltimore isn't something I see a lot, but it never ceases to amaze me when I do. Office buildings are dark, people long gone for the weekend, while the clubs and bars are just getting started. One day I'll work in a building like these. I hope, anyway.

Toni tries this every time we go out to get me some "meat," but I'm never feeling it, and tonight is no different. The last thing I want to worry about is dick. I want to have a good night with my girls, go home, and hope the hangover isn't too bad tomorrow. I haven't had a boyfriend, or any intimacy, in three years now. Even then, it was a pump-pump-squirt scenario. I don't even think he lasted two minutes.

Since then, I've been focusing on my coursework and passing all my classes. I always said once I successfully did that, then maybe I would think about dating. Toni knows a one-night stand is not a part of that plan. I'm not against them for others. I root for my girls' hook-ups all the time, it's just not for me. No real reason other than I lack the confidence I think you need for something like that. Getting naked for random guys sounds like my own personal hell. My weight is like a yo-yo, and it's left me hesitant about who I undress in front of.

Unlike my best friend. She's drop-dead gorgeous and perfect in every way. Her platinum blonde hair with thin streaks of pink matches her personality to a T. The pink streaks highlight her crazy side. She also has a very healthy sexual appetite she loves to tell me every detail about. Even goes as far as sharing any dick picture she receives with me. I'd rather she didn't, but she says it's a part of our best friend membership and it's her job to make sure I remember what dick looks like.

Most of my sexual knowledge comes from her, honestly. Unlike me, she doesn't want a long-term serious boyfriend. She likes going with the flow and blowing wherever the wind takes her. Sometimes, I wish I could be like that, but we are the perfect pair, which is why we have been best friends since being kids. We met in kindergarten, and she has been stuck by my side ever since. Whenever our parents picked schools for us to attend, we had to make sure we were at the same one, we even had vacations together. She's the Dory to my Marlin—she is one of the most forgetful people I have ever met, but I'd be lost without her. When I need help, I never have to tell her with what because she doesn't care, the answer is always yes. She's like that with everyone. Honestly, anyone with Toni in their life is extremely lucky.

Turning toward her, she's posing for the selfie mode on her phone. No doubt taking a new dating profile picture.

"Like what you see?" she says with a wink.

I throw my head back on a laugh, then, in that moment, there's a flash.

"Omg, look at this picture of you. You're so beautiful and happy, Ry. It's so good to have you back, my baby. I've missed my bestie." She glances at me with her wide golden-brown eyes.

I glimpse at the picture and genuinely smile. I do look happy. No more black bags under my eyes. I'm glowing. I smile at the screen and then wrap my arm around Toni, pull her to me, and whisper, "Because I got a best friend like you, that's why."

"I love you, Ry," she whispers, her voice muffled by my chest.

"I love you too, Ton." Then give her an extra squeeze before I let her go.

"I'll cut you if you have ruined my hair." She scowls after pulling away and immediately pulls up her phone to ensure I didn't.

God, I've missed this girl.

A neon-red sign spelling Freedom comes into view and the cab stops. I glance in Toni's direction, and she's already slapping money down and stepping out of the cab. I follow her. The icy air brushes over my exposed skin, sending a shiver up my body—November in Baltimore is freezing. As we walk in, I let out a breath I didn't realize I was holding. Having not been out for a while, and using fake IDs, I'm a bit anxious, but I can already tell this place has a good vibe. Everyone is happy, girls dancing away on the dance floor.

The bar is up high, which I love—that must be great for people-watching. The music pumps through my body, giving me the best hit of adrenaline. We've not been inside more than five minutes, not even long enough for me to toss back a single drink, when Toni is scoping out potentials for me like I didn't tell her this was a girls' night only.

"What about him, Ry? He is defo your type," she says while staring at the poor guy. I don't bother looking.

"Ton, leave it. I just want some drinks and a girls' night with you guys. Please."

She meets my eyes, grimacing and letting out a long breath that causes her shoulders to slump.

"Okay, Ry, sorry. I just wanted you to have fun, but I get it. What's more fun than a night with your girls, hmm?"

Raising my hand to give her a high-five, she slaps it, and we giggle while we walk up the stairs to the bar. Tash, Jayleigh, and Rosa are already there sipping on their drinks. As we get closer, my stomach drops at Tash's devilish smirk.

"Shots!" she shouts loud enough to be heard over the booming music. *I can already feel the hangover.*

Three shots of tequila followed by two vodka colas, and I'm most definitely feeling tipsy. "Jumpin' Jumpin'" by Destiny's Child is blaring through the speakers, and we're all dancing and singing like no one is watching, and I'm having the best time. I needed this night out to feel alive, being stuck in, constantly studying, not socializing and going out, makes you feel isolated and dead inside sometimes.

"Bathroom!" I shout and point toward the bathroom sign because I know they can't hear me over the music. They all give me the thumbs-up, except Ton who walks with me. We have always said it's an unwritten rule you can't go to the bathroom without someone. Halfway there, I get knocked back two steps by someone. Luckily, I don't fall, but I bump into a few other people whose drinks spill, followed by a couple of "What the fucks?" Then two hands grip my upper arms, and I drag my eyes up to the man towering over me. He's broad with the most beautiful ocean-blue eyes I have ever seen. Taking in his face, he has the fullest most-kissable lips and—oh my fucking God, is that a fucking nose stud?

My stomach is doing somersaults. He smells so beautiful too, like mint and expensive aftershave, electrifying my body. *Fuck. He is so hot.* I'm deep in my observation of this guy when the heat from his hands spreads like a bolt of lightning throughout my body, zapping me between the legs and leaving a dull ache—something I've never felt before, not like this. I don't know how much time has passed when I'm finally able to pull myself from admiring him. The guy stares at me, eyebrows drawn together as he makes strong eye contact. Glancing to my left, Toni grins back at me like the Cheshire cat. Behind him, three other guys look between me and their beautiful friend, a mix of confused and smirking faces.

Someone shakes me and then I realize it's Toni.

"Ry, you good?" She still has that smile on her face. The guy has let go of me and stepped back, giving Toni room to crowd me. I shake my head, the blush creeping up my face. *How embarrassing, he must think I'm a freak.* I never do stuff like this, but I can honestly say I have never seen such a beautiful man before. I brush my dress down before locking eyes with him straight away.

"I . . . I'm sorry." I try to shout loud enough so he can hear me. I can't think of anything else to say. All I know is my face is burning and I get turned on from this man touching my shoulders. I need to get away quickly. I don't intend to wait around and hear his reply, as he is still eyeing me with worry prominent on his face.

As I go to walk away, he grabs my arm and leans in and shouts, "Hey, I wanted to make sure you were okay and say sorry for bumping into you. I didn't see you, I wasn't paying attention, completely my fault." His hands are raised, but all I can concentrate on is the sexiest, husky voice that came out of his mouth. *Fuck, was this man carved from God himself?* It's actually annoying how perfect he is.

I give him a small smile and mumble, "No problem, I'm good." Then, I grab Toni's arm and walk toward the restroom, but Toni is resisting and tugging me back.

"Ry, what the fuck are you doing? There is no way we are walking away from him! Did you see the way he was eyeballing you? He was basically eating you alive with his eyes." She tries to whisper but fails miserably, because this is Toni we're talking about.

"I don't know how drunk you are, Ton, but he was definitely looking at me like I was the biggest freak he has ever met," I say while walking away from her because she has lost her mind. I'm not going back there, no matter how much she wants me to, I am mortified. I pull open the creaky stall door. The music is muffled, but my ears are still ringing. Closing my eyes, I suck in a breath and blow it back out. All I can see are those piercing blue eyes. I've never been so pulled in by someone, and of course, being the person I am, I embarrass myself right away. *How do I go back out there?* This place is big, so hopefully I won't see him for the rest of the night.

The door rattles when someone pounds on it. Thankfully, it's locked but my heart still pounds in my chest. I say nothing, hoping they realize someone is in here since the door is locked.

"Ry, which toilet are you in?" *Oh my God.*

I jump when another bang lands on my door. "Toni, stop! I'm in here."

"This one?" She bangs again.

For fuck's sake. "Yes, Ton. Give me two secs."

"No, let me in now." This girl is anything but patient. To be honest, we always use the same toilet. It's just one of those things we do. I hover and lean forward to unlock the door while swaying slightly. *God, those drinks have hit me more than I thought.*

"Why did you run off?" she says as soon as she walks in, closing and locking the door behind her.

I sigh. "Because I knew you weren't going to let it go and would try to drag me back."

"I fucking knew it," she screams.

Oh, what now? "What did you know?" She has that big grin on her face again. I wish she would stop looking at me like that, but then I realize she's not looking at me directly.

"Look at your panties, Ry."

Is this girl for real? I follow her eyes between my legs to my red panties to see what she is freaking out about. A huge wet patch. *Fuck.* I fumble with the toilet paper and wipe myself, and it easily slides through my folds. It's been a long ass time since I have been this wet. How can one touch and a set of sexy-as-fuck eyes do this? I'm not drunk enough for this.

I stand, pull my panties back in place, and move my dress back into position while avoiding Toni's heavy gaze as she takes my place on the toilet. I steal a glance, only to find her grinning at me like she can read every thought in my head. She's not going to let this go until I admit that spot was from that guy.

"Firstly, Toni, did you really have to inspect my panties, you dirty bitch."

Of course, her not giving a fuck, she just replies with a raised eyebrow.

"And secondly, Miss Observant, yes, he was hot as fuck, and I have not seen someone that beautiful in a while." She tries to cut me off, but I don't let her. "Uh-uh, let me finish for once in your life, woman. Shut up! He is beautiful, *however*, I made myself seem like a complete dick and could not possibly confront him again. I don't care what you say, Toni. I don't care how you thought he was looking at me. I'm having a good night and we are going to forget what happened out there and the God's gift I encountered. Okay?"

She glares at me as though she wants to say a whole lot of stuff, but she brings her hand to her lips and does the zip motion along her mouth.

Phew, thank God for that, she normally doesn't let stuff go, so I'm taking this as a win. She finishes, and we head out of the stall, wash our hands, and make our way back to the dance floor. I won't lie to myself and say I can't stop scanning as we walk back to the table, hoping and praying we don't bump into him. The girls are still in the same place, dancing and giggling away. They point to the bar as if they're reading my mind. I need a drink or ten, at this rate.

While we order our drinks, Cardi B comes on the speaker and the girls rush away, forgetting theirs. Not that I blame them, this song can get anyone hyped, and when Toni looks at me, her brow raised, I can't stop my laugh.

"Fitting, isn't it." Her laughter joins mine, but a voice behind me has me stopping in my tracks.

"So why is this song fitting, then?"

I stare at Toni, eyes wide, not wanting to turn around to see who is behind me. My thoughts go straight to the man from earlier, but his voice is embedded in my head—it's definitely not him. I turn around and don't recognize him. He's cute with his mousy-brown hair styled to perfection, swept back off his face. His soulless, borderline black eyes unsettle me as he studies me. As I take in his face, it's then I remember he was one of the guys standing behind Blue Eyes earlier, which I'm assuming is his friend. Oh God. I laugh it off and wave my hand in front of me.

"Oh, just a joke," I say to him, smiling. He smirks at me, as if he knows it is not a joke, but he doesn't push.

He places his hand out. "Well, it's nice to meet you, I'm James." He flashes me a dazzling white smile, which shows off his straight white teeth, while moving closer. He has to be at least six foot, if not more, and the way he towers over me has me stepping back. I shake his hand and offer him a polite smile. "I'm Rylee and this is my friend, Toni."

"Best friend!" I roll my eyes at her, and he laughs.

"Well, it's nice to meet you, "Best friend Toni," he jokes.

We both laugh, and he offers to buy us a drink. Before I can even say no, as we just had our drinks delivered, Toni has listed what we are drinking with added shots. This girl has no shame. James calls over the bartender while Toni downs her drink and nudges me to do the same. I side-eye James to make sure he's not watching us, because it feels awkward, although, I'm sure he sees our drinks in front of us anyway.

As our drinks are delivered, Ton snatches hers straight away and downs the shot. I down mine after, and it's then I realize James is staring at me. He has moved closer and is making me uncomfortable. Don't get me wrong, he's a handsome guy, but not my type. He seems nice enough, but there's just something about him that's off. It's just a feeling.

"Thanks for the drinks, James," I say as I turn to Toni but bump into someone before I can get her to go to the dance floor again.

I mutter an apology, and before walking off, I hear that voice.

"I bumped into you, you bumped into me. I don't feel as bad now, we can call it even."

I swear I feel his voice between my legs. *Is that a thing?* Who knew? It's Blue Eyes smirking down with the most panty-wetting smile. Literally. The laugh that comes out of me is not something I have heard come from me before. It's between a little girl's giggle and a hyena. *Kill me now.*

"Before you run away from me again, are you going to let me buy you a drink to say sorry for earlier?" Before I can even reply, James pipes up from behind me.

"Already brought her a drink, Jay." James sounds irritated but tries to pass it off as friendly. I don't know if Jay notices, but he doesn't even glance at James, just keeps his eyes on me.

"Well, I would like to buy the beautiful girl another drink." He nods at me, as if to ask, *Is that okay*?

"She would love another drink," Toni says over my shoulder. I don't think I could say no to him, he's so intense—in a good way. What I like most is that Jay keeps his eyes on me, waiting for me to say yes. I smile while looking down and nod. *Who am I, accepting two drinks from two guys within two minutes of each other.*

I turn back around to lean against the bar. Blue Eyes leans beside me and waves the bartender over, and he rattles off what he and James are drinking and then looks at me. I say what I'm having, Toni adds in what she is having with a side shot, of course. James then shouts to make those four shots. *Fuck, I don't know how much more alcohol I can handle.*

Toni nudges my side, and she whispers in my ear, "Remind me to take you out more often." We giggle loudly and then Blue Eyes asks us to share the joke. I hold eye contact while fluttering my eyelashes, trying to muster an innocent look, which makes him laugh.

He leans in while placing his hand on my hip and whispers, "Sorry, I didn't introduce myself, I'm Jace." I swear his lips brush my ear—my clit certainly thinks it did, it's fucking pulsing.

What is this guy doing to me? Jace, not Jay. Jace suits him, it's sexy but also bold, and I couldn't think of better fitting words to describe him. I gather myself and try to control my breathing.

I lean my head back, as he's still close, and stare into his eyes. They're just too beautiful not to look at. They stand out more against his pale skin and short, dark brown hair.

"I'm Rylee, it's nice to meet you, Jace." His warm smile, framed by the sexiest stubbled beard, lights up his face.

"Cringe line coming, but your name really is beautiful, which, of course, matches you," he says while scratching his head with his lips tipped up in a half smile.

I throw my head back on a laugh. The drinks are hitting me more than I realized, and I try flirting by following up with "That is a cringe line, but out of your mouth, it's not." Heat creeps into my cheeks. *I can't believe I said that.*

Before Jace can say anything, James says—sounding slightly annoyed over Jace's shoulder—he is going back to their table. Jace turns around and nods.

"Someone's pissed they didn't win the girl," Toni chimes in.

"Oh, did I get the girl, then?" Jace says, making me jump. I roll my eyes at Toni.

"Just ignore her, I normally do."

"Rude," Toni mumbles. I wink at her, and she kisses my cheek while backing away.

"I'm heading back to the girls, I need to shake this ass and find me some meat. Ciao, babes."

I glare at Toni as she walks off while raising her brows at me with a shit-eating grin on her face. *I can't believe she has left me here on my own.*

"Did she just say 'find me some meat'?" Jace says through a laugh.

"She did, I'm sure you realized in those few minutes of meeting her, she does not mince her words." Jace laughs and takes a sip of his drink.

"I did notice, it can be refreshing though. I'm sure she keeps you entertained."

"Oh, she does."

A slight smirk graces Jace's lips as he tilts his head to the side, eyeing me, causing fireworks to go off inside my body. I can't believe a guy can make me feel like this so soon. *What the fuck?*

"You know, you really are beautiful, Rylee. I'm praying you're not going to tell me you have a boyfriend." Jace takes another sip of his drink, eyeing me over his cup while waiting for me to answer.

"What if I said I did?"

"Then I'd say, that's a damn shame . . . for him." He smirks.

"Why him?"

"Because he won't be the one you're waking up to," he says with a full-blown grin. The heat that surges through my body has me standing there lost for words. It feels like he's staring through my soul, and the heat penetrating from his eyes like laser beams burns through my skin. My mouth goes dry as I struggle to swallow.

"I need another drink; I would now like to buy you one as an apology for bumping into you." I bet he wanted me to come back with a sexy remark, but me and sexy do not belong in the same sentence. At least I didn't laugh like a hyena again—silver linings, I guess.

Jace flashes the perfect smile, which shows off his gorgeous white straight teeth. *Can you fall in love this early?*

"Why not. I'll have a Jack and Coke."

Jace and I have been chatting at the bar and drinking, and the next thing I know, an hour has gone by. We have been talking about everything and nothing. Jace stands and looks toward the dance floor.

"I think your friends and my friends have found each other; they're all on the dance floor. Do you want to head down?"

"Yeah, why not. I'm sure the girls will bitch me out if I don't go back to them soon." I stand but don't realize how drunk I am and topple to the left, and Jace catches me.

"Oh my God, I'm so sorry, that is so embarrassing. I didn't realize how drunk I was." I giggle and hiccup at the same time.

"Come on, let's get you back to your friends before they accuse me of trying to get you drunk on purpose."

As we walk down the stairs, I realize how drunk I am, but I'm feeling amazing and want to dance. As soon as we get near the girls, I grab Jace's hand and wrap it around my waist so it rests just above my bikini line. I back into his front and start to move with him. He wraps his other hand around my front, laying it flat on my belly. Bringing his lips to the side of my neck, he gently kisses it, sending a shiver down my spine. He smiles into my neck, telling me he felt that shiver. I grind on him, and his erection hits my lower back. He doesn't even try to hide it, which I like. Jace has this confidence about him, not a cocky confidence, a sexy confidence. I don't even pay attention to anyone else, all I can feel, think, and smell is him.

"Rylee," he whispers in my ear and keeps his head there so he can hear me.

"Yes?"

"Where are you going when you leave here?"

"Home, why?"

"I'm going to ask this again, and you're going to answer me correctly," he says as his lips skim my ear.

My heart is coming out of my chest, he wants me to go back to his. *Oh my God, can I do this?*

"Rylee, where are you going when you leave here?"

I don't even need to think, the wetness between my legs from having him in my proximity for half the night has answered this for me.

"Yours," I gasp out.

He smiles into my neck.

"That's the correct answer, baby," he says before placing an open-mouthed kiss on my neck, which has my eyes rolling back in my head.

We dance more and get more drinks. Our group is mingling now, and Toni will not stop looking at me with the biggest smile on her face, and I have to say, I can't help but return it. I feel so happy, it's probably the alcohol, but I don't even care. I'm having the best night.

The DJ comes over the speaker, giving us our warning for last drinks before closing. Toni comes up to me and says it's best we leave now, otherwise it will be a nightmare getting a taxi if we leave when everyone else does.

When we get outside, the air hits me and I feel like I have downed five drinks at once. My vision is distorted, and I try my best to act normal. I already told the girls I was going back to Jace's, to which they screamed the club down, so they know I will jump in a taxi with him. Toni made me turn my location on and share it with her via WhatsApp and even took Jace's ID so she could get his address. She is good like that, she is wild, but she is also the protective momma bear that every girl needs.

Jace waves down a taxi, and I turn to the girls and give them all a kiss goodbye. I'm trying too hard to walk in a straight line, but I stumble slightly as we approach the taxi. Jace catches me and guides me into the car, and James slides in after him. I'm trying too hard to concentrate on keeping myself composed to be worried as to why he got in the taxi with us.

"You okay, Rylee, you're a bit pale?" I turn to the right, and James is leaning forward so he can see past Jace.

"Mm," I mumble, because honestly, I feel so spaced out and sick, I can't dare to open my mouth.

They're talking but it's like I'm far away from them. I lean my head back against the seat, hoping if I just close my eyes, I will feel better once I open them.

"Rylee, Rylee . . ."

I peel my eyes open, everything is blurry, so I close them again, and my head is killing me.

"Rylee, babe, can you open your eyes for me?"

"Mm, I can't," I murmur. "My head hurts too much."

I lay my head back against what I can only assume is the headrest before I let the blackness take me.

My head hurts so much as I flicker my eyes open but instantly close them again. *God, I feel like death. How much did I drink last night? My mouth feels like cotton, I need some water.* I sit up without even opening my eyes, and then freeze. My eyes snap open, the loudest gasp leaves my body.

"Where the fuck am I?" I look down. I'm in a man's shirt at least five sizes too big for me that covers my thighs.

I sit there, squeezing my eyes closed, trying to think over the thumping in my head. *Fuck . . . Jace.* I look around at the modern spacious white room. It doesn't seem like a man's room, nor a woman's room, it's very neutral. I really hope this is Jace's room.

Faint whistling comes from outside the room as I comb my fingers through my hair. There's clumps of hair stuck together. *What the fuck is that from?* There isn't a mirror, so God knows how awful I look, but I need to know what happened last night. I head out of the room and follow the whistling. I pass multiple doors before I come to an open-plan kitchen. A shiver runs through my body as my eyes land on a topless Jace cooking and whistling with the stereo on at a low volume. I don't make myself known, instead I admire how amazing his body is.

He's ripped with the sexiest V and beautiful abs. My eyes glide down to the line of hair that disappears into the waistband of his gray joggers, which has my thighs clenching together.

I'm interrupted from admiring him when he clears his throat. I glance up at him, the smile he has on his face is like nothing I have seen before. He's like he was made from God himself and then passed down for the angels to complete him. His smile has my stomach swarming with butterflies and my pussy throbbing.

"Morning, babe, you feeling okay?" he says while walking over to me with a cup in his hand. He passes me the cup, and I haven't answered him because I'm trying to pick my jaw up off the floor. Being this close to him, he is good enough to fucking eat on the spot.

It then dawns on me that he's asking if I feel okay because of the state I was in last night. I remember getting into the taxi and nothing after that. My cheeks are burning as I drop my gaze to the floor and whisper, "I'm sorry." I'm so mortified I could cry. He doesn't need silly girls who don't know how to handle their alcohol, he could get any girl he wanted. I want to get out of here and never have to face him again, even though the thought of that sends a punch to my gut.

I mumble another quick apology and head back to his room. Hopefully he will be happy I'm walking away and will leave me to grab my stuff and go. I'm looking around his room when he enters abruptly. He paces over to me, his eyes drawn together.

"Hey, what's wrong, you don't need to be sorry."

"Do you know where my clothes are?" I rush out. "I will get changed and head home, I don't remember what happened last night, but all I can say is I'm sorry and you don't need to worry about seeing me again. If you can just get me my clothes, I'll be on my way."

"Your clothes are in the dryer. I put them in the wash last night and then put them in the dryer this morning," Jace says, his features softening. As I'm wondering why the hell he is washing my clothes, he reaches out, placing a hand gently on my shoulder.

"You are not going anywhere until you have something to eat, which is nearly ready, and drink some water. I want to make sure you're okay, Rylee," he says with a softer tone. I give him a small smile, but I'm confused as to why he's being so nice. I'm a random girl he met on a night out and now he's washing my clothes. *Wait . . .*

"Why are you washing my clothes, did I fall over or something?" I ask.

He brings his hand to the back of his neck and rubs it, casting his eyes around the room.

"You were a little sick when we got inside, you couldn't walk from the taxi and wouldn't keep your eyes open, so I carried you in and laid you down in my bed. You then sat up and got sick down yourself and on me a little bit. I had to undress you, but I swear nothing else happened, I wouldn't touch you in an inappropriate way while you were like that," he rushes out, without taking a breath.

I gasp and bring my hand to my mouth. "Jace," I say into my hand. I don't even know what to say right now. *How can he even have me in his house right now?*

"Jace, I'm totally mortified, I'm so, so sorry. I will pay for whatever dry cleaning you need to do. I feel awful." Jace laughs and brushes it off.

"Don't worry yourself, babe, we have all been there. Plus, I think it will be a good story to tell the grandkids," he says with a wink and a bold smile.

"You what, grandkids?" I step back, eyes bulging.

Jace throws his head back on a laugh. "You should see your face right now. I'm joking, of course," he says sarcastically, which makes me think he isn't joking, but he must be because who on earth would want kids with me with the state I'm in.

"Let's get some food in you before you go anywhere." He looks at me with puppy-dog eyes. "Please." He sticks his bottom lip out.

I chuckle and give him a quick nod.

After eating, Jace loads up the dishwasher while I sit there playing with the ends of the shirt I'm wearing. He turns and says he can drop me home once he's finished, to which I let out a breath I didn't even realize I was holding.

"Don't appear so pleased to be leaving me." He pulls a sad face.

"I just feel a bit grim. I want to get home, freshen up, and die in bed all day," I say with an awkward laugh.

"Nah, I get it. Your clothes should be dry." He grabs them out of the dryer and passes them to me. I thank him and head back to his room.

I must ask him what softener he uses; it smells amazing.

Once dressed, I head back out into the kitchen, feeling a bit awkward dressed back in the clothes I was wearing last night. Jace did offer to lend me a pair of joggers and a top but there is no way he will want to see me again after today, and I won't want his clothes as a memory of how embarrassing I was.

Jace is standing against his kitchen counter, looking as beautiful as ever, which makes me more conscious as I have my hair up in a bun on top of my head and last night's makeup on. Luckily, the waterproof mascara is life and still looks pretty good.

"You ready?" he says while eyeing me. The ache between my legs reminds me I never even got to touch or kiss him. The sexual tension in here could slice through ice.

I nod because I don't trust opening my mouth. With the way I'm feeling, I could fuck him right here, right now, but I feel dirty and haven't even brushed my teeth, as Jace couldn't find a spare toothbrush. Smirking as if he knows what he's doing, he turns and grabs his keys off the kitchen counter.

"Let's go, then, beautiful," he says, throwing his keys up in the air and catching them.

I follow Jace out to his car and head toward his BMW. He opens the passenger door for me, and I raise a brow at him but take a seat inside. I have to wonder what this guy does for a living. *This has to be the newest model.*

Jace jumps in the car and starts the engine.

"You good to direct me from here?" he asks.

"Yeah, just head toward the mall, I can direct you from there," I say, blushing.

I'm staring out the window, feeling a little awkward in the silence, but I have no idea what to even say. Thankfully, Jace interrupts my thoughts.

"I didn't even ask you how old you were?" He laughs awkwardly. "That probably should have been something I asked before taking you home, hey?"

I grin. "Yes, it should have"—I raise my brow at him—"but you're safe, don't worry. I'm twenty, how old are you?" I question.

"Don't worry, you're safe too, I'm twenty-one," he shoots back with a grin.

"Then we're both safe and no one will be getting arrested today," I say, trying to be serious but end up laughing, to which Jace follows.

"Well, technically, no rules would have been broken, anyway," he points out.

"Okay, yes, don't remind me of my exorcist audition last night, please." I wince.

Jace roars out in laughter.

"That was a good one, but it wasn't quite that bad, don't worry."

He has made me feel at ease, even if he wasn't trying. The rest of the journey is in comfortable silence, apart from me telling him where to go.

"Well, this is me," I say, turning to Jace.

He bends his head slightly to look at the entrance to my apartment block.

"Let me walk you to the door," he says, getting out of the car before I can tell him not to worry. I want this awkwardness to be over so I never have to see him again, even though the thought of that makes me disappointed. We walk side by side to the entrance doors. Needing to get this over with, I spin around.

"I know I won't be seeing you again but thank you for dropping me home, and again, I'm so sorry for last night. I honestly don't drink a lot, so when I do, it doesn't agree with me."

Jace laughs, shaking his head. He stares into my eyes and grabs a loose bit of hair, tucking it behind my ear before leaning in closer.

"You will be seeing me again, don't worry about that." He smirks while backing away, walking back to his car.

A big grin spreads across my face and fireworks go off in the pit of my stomach.

"Fuck," I breathe out.

Chapter One

Present Day

After applying the last of my makeup, I step back, assessing myself. Some days I can barely bring myself to stand in front of the mirror, but other days, I put in some effort and make myself appear half decent. I grab the oversized black blazer—since I'm conscious of my hips—and slip it on over my red spaghetti-strap top. I'm wearing black wet-look jeans. I'm not skinny but I wouldn't class myself as overweight. I'm a comfortable size twelve, but I'm sure at least half of my weight sits in my hips. I'm happy with my weight. Am I ecstatic? No, but who is. I have cellulite and stretch marks. Girls don't realize that even the skinniest girls have them, most people do, and it's not something you can help, but I understand why people are embarrassed by them. I rub my body in bio-oil some days and then other days I don't give a shit. We're girls, we will never be happy with our bodies, no matter what we look like.

I walk out of my en suite bathroom and into my closet to grab a pair of pointed-heel pumps. Heeled shoes are a godsend. It can change a whole outfit, especially five-inch heels. I slip them on and glance up, staring at myself in the full-length body mirror attached to my closet.

"So beautiful."

I spin around to find my gorgeous boyfriend leaning against the doorframe, looking me up and down.

"Jace, you scared the shit out of me."

He stalks toward me, grabbing my hips and pulling me in, trying to kiss me, but I dodge him.

"Ah ah, I just did my lipstick, you are not ruining it."

Jace groans as he kisses up my neck.

"Do we have to go out, Ry. I would much rather stay in and watch you strip out of this outfit."

I shuffle out of his hold. "You know we have to go, we can't not."

It's then I get a good look at Jace. He's to die for in his fitted dark-blue jeans and white fitted Ralph Lauren tee that highlights his broad shoulders and muscular arms. *Maybe staying home would be the better option.*

"You sure I can't persuade you?" He smirks, knowing the way he's dressed is doing things to me. I snap out of my haze.

"C'mon, we are going, I'm not staying in this house with you one minute longer. Bridget put a lot of effort into this meal today."

"You did pick up your dad's present from the kitchen side, didn't you?" I ask Jace while he drives us to the restaurant for his dad's birthday meal.

"Yes, I did. I also picked up the banners that Bridge asked us to bring." *Oops, I forgot about those.* Jace is way more organized than I am.

"Oh, well done, you know how unorganized I am." I smile sweetly at him.

He laughs. "I definitely do, Ry."

I roll my eyes at him and then take a minute to appreciate how fucking sexy he is. I always watch Jace and think how lucky I am. Who knew that night in the club would bring me here, with him, now. How Jace still wanted to speak to me after that, I will never know, but I could not be happier that he did.

I still remember receiving a call the night after he dropped me home. He was the perfect gentleman and wanted to take me out for an official date, which we did, and I had this instant connection with him. We live together in his, now our, apartment and are in a perfect, happy relationship. It's crazy how someone so perfect can walk into your life when, one, you're not expecting it, and two, you don't actually want it.

I run my gaze over his face. I love watching him drive. All ladies can agree how hot it is to watch a man drive, especially when driving with one hand firmly holding your thigh while rubbing circles and the other holding the wheel. Their arms just pop. All the veins and the muscles showing. Just like Jace now. After all this time, I still get butterflies and tingles between my legs while watching him. As if reading my mind, he smirks and flicks his beautiful blue eyes to me, and I can see the lust there. It's like we're one person, and whatever I feel, he feels it too.

"You good, babe?" he says with a sly smirk.

"Yes, course I am. Why wouldn't I be?" I blurt.

"I don't know, maybe because your legs have my hand in a death grip."

Oh. Oops. I open my legs a bit so he can remove his hand, but he uses the opportunity to move his hand farther up, resting it on the crease of my bikini line. I close my eyes, trying to calm my racing heart. Maybe he doesn't realize what he's doing and it's just me.

He knows exactly what he's doing when he grazes his pinky finger over the seam of my jeans directly over my center. He's not applying pressure but the ghost of a touch has me craving more.

"Jace, what are you doing, concentrate on driving, we will be at the restaurant soon," I say, breathless. As turned on as I am, I don't think this is the best idea while he's driving.

"You worry too much, babe." He smiles and then removes his hand, only to bring it up to my high-waist jeans and undo the button. Before I can even say anything, his hand is pushing past the waistline of my panties. The minute his fingers touch my pussy, he smiles. "Ry. You're fucking soaked, what have you been thinking about?" He runs his fingers through my slit, grazing my clit, causing my breath to hitch. My whole body is craving him now. I can't believe he is doing this while driving, but if he stopped, I would scream.

I glance up at Jace, he keeps his eyes on the road with one hand controlling the wheel. I move my legs to the left to give him better access. If he won't stop, I want to at least make it easier for him, as our safety is also at risk here.

"Answer me, baby, what were you thinking about?" he rasps.

I gasp as he pushes two fingers inside me. I try to ride his fingers, as I can already hear how wet I am. Then I realize I haven't answered him. "I was wa-watching you—oh god—driving and reveling in how sexy you are," I say as quickly as possible because I'm losing my breath. He pushes two fingers as deep inside me as he can go, hooking them at the right angle, causing goose bumps to erupt down my body. It's not going to be long, the pressure is already building in the core of my stomach.

"Do you know how sexy you are, beautiful girl?" His seductive voice fills the car. The heel of his palm rubbing against my clit. I glide my hips up and down, shamelessly rubbing myself against his palm. "I want you to come, Rylee, I want your cum running down my fingers. When we're at the restaurant, I want to be able to smell your juices on me while I'm eating."

"Oh, fuck. Ja-ce, don't stop." While holding his arm in place, my orgasm hits me hard. I can't catch my breath. Jace slowly pushes his fingers in and out while I ride out the orgasm.

"That's it, baby, I can't wait to get you home later. There was no way I could wait until then for a taste," he says as he pulls his fingers out of my jeans and brings them to his lips, licking them clean.

I swear he gets hotter by the day. While I come down from my orgasm, it hits me how dangerous but also how hot that was. I glance down at his lap and see the bulge in his pants. I smirk to myself, thinking of all the ways I can pay him back later.

Pulling up in the restaurant lot, I flip down the sun visor and flip the mirror open to check my makeup and hair before getting out. I wipe under my eyes and run my fingers through my hair. I'm flushed, but I can blame that on the weather, it's January and is freezing in Baltimore.

"You're beautiful as always, babe," Jace says while grabbing his dad's present from the back seat.

"I still can't believe you did that while driving, Jace."

"I'm pretty sure I heard you say, 'Don't stop, Jace'?" He pulls a serious face like he is trying to remember something. I laugh and punch him in the arm. He throws his head back on a laugh and gets out of the car. I step out also and spot Jace's Aunt Bridget getting balloons out of her car.

"Hey, Bridge," I say as we approach the car.

Jace gives her a hug and kisses her head. She wraps her arms around Jace's waist and squeezes him.

"I have missed you both so much, it feels like forever since I have seen you," she mumbles into Jace's chest. It's funny seeing them together, Jace with his six-foot-three self dwarfs Bridget's five-foot frame. She is so dinky, and from the back, you would think she was a child. However, she is beautiful, you would never in your life think she is forty-three, she is slim but curvy and is always styled in the latest fashion, always wearing heels and looks immaculate. People that didn't know her would probably think she was a bit stuck-up, but it couldn't be any further from the truth. She is one of the nicest and caring ladies I have ever encountered. I feel lucky to have her in my life. She also adores Jace as if he were her own.

Jace takes the balloons from her while I grab a few other party bits out of the trunk.

"Thank you, my beautiful girl," she says while grabbing my face with both hands and giving me a kiss on each cheek.

Her kind big blue eyes stare back at me, creasing in the corners from her big smile. I class Bridget as my own aunt, she's made me feel comfortable from day one. She is the fun, cool aunt with no kids and just lives her life carefree while going on loads of holidays each year. She lives her best life when not working and has always said she has no regrets not having children, not that she couldn't have them now at forty-three, but she likes doing things spontaneously and not having anyone to care for. I respect her for that.

"Something about you is different, Bridge, but I can't pinpoint what it is." I step back, scanning her from head to toe.

She smirks while standing there, letting me take her in. When my eyes trail back to her face, I notice the two ash-blond sweeps hanging down and around her heart-shaped face.

"Oh my God," I say, "your hair!"

"Do you like it?" She beams and grabs her long glossy hair from behind her and brings it around her delicate shoulders as it cascades down her front, hitting just below her waistline.

"Bridge, I love the colors, is it low lights? I love the layers too!" I gush while running my hands through the long straight strands. I keep staring at the mix of blonde and brown, imagining what

I would look like with some blonde highlights through my dark brown hair.

"It is. Ken did such a good job of it." As if reading my mind, she follows up with "He could do yours too, Ry. It would make those gorgeous bluey-green eyes of yours stand out more." Ken has always been Bridget's hairdresser. I have met him a couple of times at some of Bridget's parties, as they have a close friendship. I could have sworn something was going on with them once, but she assured me he was gay. However, the way his eyes followed Bridge every time she walked, I would say he's bi.

"Mine does need some TLC, and this is stunning, Bridge. I can't stop running my fingers through it, it's like I'm touching silk. The way it gleams is beautiful."

"Hmm, lets see what your birthday brings." She winks at me and walks toward the restaurant doors.

Chapter 2

Walking into the restaurant, Jace has already made them aware that we are here under the reservation Bridget booked. We are shown to our table, which is in a private room set out at the back of the restaurant, hidden away. The setup is beautiful, the rectangular table with two bottles of champagne cooling in ice, and jugs of water set out down the middle. There are glass windows surrounding us, flooding the room with natural light. To the left is a set of double doors which would open up onto a beautiful large garden, it's a shame it's not summer in Baltimore. Otherwise, having those open with the sunshine would be amazing, but no, it's like the Antarctica outside. It's still a lovely view while we eat.

I glance at my phone to see how long we have until Jace's dad turns up with the rest of his family. "Okay, we got ten minutes until he gets here, Bridget, what can I do?" Bridget hands me some table confetti which says *Happy Birthday* and asks me to scatter it across the table, then hands Happy Birthday banners and tape to Jace and asks him to put them up on the walls surrounding our table. I glance over at Jace and smirk. He's already side-eyeing me with a flat smile, trying to hold his laugh in. Bridget is sticking balloons on the walls and even has some helium ones to tie to the back of his dad's chair.

I personally can't wait to see his face, it will be the same moody frown as always. I think I have only ever seen him smile a handful of times. Jace works with him so sees him most days and says he's fine. I told Jace it must be me, but he thinks I'm being oversensitive and said everyone has their days. Weirdly enough, when I first met Jace's dad, he held a conversation with me. He's always been the quiet type, the type that sits back and observes, but he was at least nice and made me feel welcome. That changed after being with Jace for about a year. I mentioned it to Jace, but he shrugged it off and blamed it on work. Five years later, and nothing has changed. Jace gets along with him and that's all that matters, but it would be nice for him to at least try and act like he likes me instead of making it awkward.

"Oh, fuck" comes from behind me, and I spin around and Jace's uncle is standing there with a big grin on his face, taking in all the decorations. He drags his eyes to Bridget, trying to hold down his laugh.

"Bridge, you know he is not going to like this."

Shrugging, she says, "Tough, he can get over it, it's not every day your big brother turns forty-five, and I want to make sure he knows it." She smirks.

I shake my head, laughing while walking over to Boh, wrapping my arms around his waist, I tip my head back, looking up his face. He flashes his straight white teeth, looking down at me, and pulls me in for the tightest hug. Boh and I got along from the minute we met, he is the total opposite to his moody brother and actually treats me like family.

"I have missed you, kid," Boh says while squeezing me tighter.

Boh is, in all honesty, gorgeous, like all the men in Jace's family. Tall, dark, handsome, and they all have these piercing blue eyes that stand out in every room they are in. However, Boh is the more-rugged type out of the boys. He has tattoos covering both arms that wrap around his chest. He has this bad-boy look to him, but he's anything but. Boh is one of the sweetest men I have had the pleasure of meeting. Although, Jace said when he needs to, he has a different side, but I have yet to see this side, not that I want to, I love Boh's sweet and cheeky side. I give him a playful frown. "That is not my fault, you never come see us at the apartment anymore."

"I know. You know what work is like. It takes over and the days fly by. I will come see you both soon." I cast my eyes down his chest and step back slightly, but he still holds on to me with an arm hanging beside me.

"Red suits you. I don't think I have seen you in it before." He is wearing a red Henley with the sleeves rolled up slightly to show off the busy art on his arms.

Jace walks over, grabs me by the waist, and pulls my back to his front.

"Hands off my woman." Jace laughs while he and Boh slap each other on the shoulder.

"It was your Mrs. checking me out. Telling me I suit red." He winks at me.

I shake my head while rolling my eyes and walk over to Bridget, leaving Jace and Boh to catch up. They all work together at Jace's dad's company, so they see each other all the time. They are always talking work, even though I tell Jace he needs to have a break when he's out of the office, but they are all devoted to that company.

As I approach Bridget, ready to ask if everything is sorted, there's a laugh at the door, and I turn, and a stunning girl walks in, wearing a royal-blue knee-length dress, which is basically second skin to her legs that are up to her neck, and long blonde waves, which go to her waist. She is stunning. Like drop-dead stunning. My stare is broken when a hand glides around her tiny waist and she steps back to reveal Jace's dad. Cash Stiles. Cash looks every bit the moody asshole he normally does but with a beautiful woman on his arm this time.

Cash stands there, oozing confidence, yet he has this air of isolation surrounding him. He is devilishly handsome with his square jawline and compelling blue eyes framed with dark long lashes that have women dropping to their knees everywhere he is. He angles his head downward from his tall, lean frame to the woman by his side and flashes her his rare smile that highlights his age lines around his eyes and mouth. She glides her hand up and runs her fingers through his stubbled beard before pushing on her tiptoes and planting a gentle kiss on his lips.

I have never seen this woman before but it's not surprising. Cash always has a new flavor of the week. Boh calls Cash's girls that, as they literally change every week, and it just stuck. Cash hates it, so I automatically love it. Cash takes in the room while his flavor of the week stands there grinning like a puppet. My eyes slide back to Cash, his defined jaw tenses, a frown appears on his face, and then his eyes zero in on Bridget.

"Happy Birthday, my dear brother," Bridget sings while walking over to Cash with open arms to give him a hug. Cash hugs her back but you can tell by his face, he's not happy. He whispers something in her ear, but I'm too far away to hear what he says. By the way Bridget rolls her eyes and steps back from him, he said something shitty. *What a surprise.*

Cash and his girlfriend, or whoever she is, walks farther into the room. Her waves bounce around her large boobs as she sways her hips. She moves like I imagine a dancer would, elegant and perfect posture. *Interesting.* Boh comes up to Cash next and goes in for their brotherly hug. Although they are different, they get along well. Boh moves his eyes over to the leggy blonde.

"Flave, nice to meet you," he says with a grin on his face. Bridget and I are trying to hide our laughs, so I have to turn around. Cash tells Boh to "Shut the fuck up," but the girl speaks up.

"Flave?" She looks at Cash and then Boh with her head tilted.

Cash huffs in annoyance, telling her to ignore Boh, then introduces her as his girlfriend Becky. Cash has never introduced a girl as his girlfriend before, so something must be different here. He never keeps his hands on them either, and he has not taken his hands off her belted waist, which highlights just how tiny it is. He places a kiss on her nose. I find Jace's eyes straight away, and even his eyebrows are raised to his hairline. Cash has never shown a woman affection in front of anyone. Cash pulls himself away as Jace and I introduce ourselves. Bridget leans in, giving Becky a kiss on her cheek. Jace turns his attention to Cash.

"Happy Birthday, old man," Jace says as they lean in for a hug and slap each other on the back.

"Hold back on the old man," Cash mumbles, breaking through with a slight smirk. He must be ill with all the little smiles he is flashing today. Okay, that is a slight exaggeration, he smiles, just not a lot.

Cash's attention turns to me, and he leans forward, sliding his hand around my waist, giving me a side kiss to my cheek.

"Rylee, how are you?" I freeze, a bit taken back. I don't think Cash has ever asked how I am. *What has Becky been putting in his drink at night?* He drops his hand, stepping back but waiting for an answer.

"I'm good, thanks," I rush out. "Oh, Happy Birthday." I smile as sweetly as I can, trying not to show my shock, because I think he felt me freeze when he asked me how I was.

Jace takes a seat next to Bridge, so I follow, taking a seat next to him. As soon as my bum hits the seat, Jace's arm is slung around the back of the chair. He always makes me feel safe, wanted. It's a secure feeling I never knew I needed. I lean into Jace as much as the chair will allow me to, without hanging off my chair. I love being close to him.

The waiter walks over, and we order our drinks. I'm driving, so I keep it to water, but I ask if he can provide me with a glass and lemon slices. Water with lemon and ice is amazing. Jace thinks I'm weird for how much I love water, but if I'm not drinking alcohol, it's water or coffee. I wouldn't be able to go through my day without coffee, only psychos do that. Jace orders a beer and so do the other guys. Bridge orders a gin and tonic, which is her signature drink. It suits her. I always think of gin and tonic as an elegant drink, and Bridget is an elegant woman. Becky orders a wine to which Cash tells the waiter to bring the bottle.

Boh asks Becky what she does for work, but before I can hear what she says, Bridget speaks to me and Jace.

"Have you two decided on a vacation?" she asks.

Bridget goes away on vacation all the time. She is an interior designer but has a rich client, so she gets paid well for the jobs she does. They can be extremely demanding, so she has to have the patience of a saint working for them, but she can take whatever time off she wants. Well, to an extent. I remember she had one client—a senior partner for a huge law firm out in New York—and he would ring Bridget all hours of the morning. It was ridiculous, but she's good at what she does. She is in such demand that she has to turn people away.

"No, we keep saying we are going to book, but we never do." Jace frowns at me like it's my fault we don't book.

I poke him in the ribs with my mouth wide. "Don't you dare look at me like that's my fault, Mr. Workaholic over here."

Jace gives me a side smile. I know he's trying to wind me up, he never gives himself time off.

"Jace, how many times have I told you"—Bridge slaps his arm—"you need to take some time off work and take your beautiful girlfriend away."

"Cash," Bridge says across the table, not caring she is interrupting Cash, Boh, and Becky. His eyes slide to Bridget, softening the minute they land on her. They have always had a close relationship. Cash being the eldest, I was told by Boh, looked out for Bridge a lot. I can imagine Boh did too. Although, Boh has joked in the past about how much of a handful Bridge was growing up. It doesn't surprise me at all.

"You need to allow your son to have some time off so he can take his girlfriend on a nice vacation."

"Jace knows he can have whatever time off he wants. He doesn't need to ask me." Cash takes a sip of his beer, keeping his eyes firmly on Jace.

"I know, I know." He sighs. "I have no excuse." He grabs my hand. "We will book something soon, I promise you."

I lean forward slightly and kiss his lips gently. "I'll hold you to that," I whisper.

We have all finished our food. I went with chicken pot pie, as I'm fussy with meat, but everyone seemed to enjoy what they had. The boys have moved around the table to talk football and work, which me and Bridge were quick to duck away from.

Becky seems like a nice girl, and we found out she met Cash at her job, a bar in the city. Not one I have heard of but there are a lot of bars in Baltimore. She explained how her and Cash were talking over the bar and he offered to walk her home at closing. She didn't go into too much detail, but I can gather what happened next.

We continue talking, Becky asks me about how I met Jace, and I replay what happened, which had Becky laughing. Bridget loves hearing the story, it never gets old. Becky also asked what Bridget and I do for work and seemed very interested in Bridget's interior design business.

I glance over at the boys on the other side of the table as the waiter approaches with a tray of shots. When he places the tray down, I see the salt and lemon. Tequila, the Stiles men's favorite. I told Jace I would drive so he could have a drink for his dad's birthday; he has been working crazy hours, so he deserves to unwind.

"Rylee," Bridge says, snapping me out of my daydream. I move my eyes back to her.

"Yes?" I smile.

"I was just saying to Becky, we should all go out for brunch sometime. It would be nice to get to know her more."

Bridge must be getting the same feeling I do—whatever is going on between her and Cash, it isn't a fling. I have noticed Cash glimpsing at her a few times in the last half hour, and he's content for once. Which is not a look Cash Stiles normally portrays.

"Sounds great, just text me a time and place and I'll be there." I smile at Bridge and Becky.

I peek back over to the boys. They all seem so happy. Cash is smiling a lot today, and as much as I think it's to do with the alcohol, something tells me Becky has a lot to do with it too.

"They look so happy," Bridge says.

"They do," I breathe out.

Jace peers up at me in the moment and smiles. The butterflies flutter in my stomach like they always do.

"You two are the cutest," Becky interrupts my thoughts.

I smile at her, blushing because she caught me staring.

"You look at him like he hung the moon and the stars for you."

Jace smiling will give any girl butterflies. His larger-than-life smile makes me weak. I think about what Becky said, Jace always has been the light in my life. Even in the dark, he shines through and guides me.

"He did. He still does."

Chapter 3

"C'mon, big guy, let's get you into bed." I try to support Jace as I sit him down on the bed.

"I feel sick." Jace groans.

Jace drops himself back on the bed like a deadweight and lies there with his eyes closed. How I got him out of the car and into the apartment, I will never know. It should have taken two minutes but turned into ten, as I was trying to support his weight while he was pushing me into walls when he couldn't stand or walk properly.

"Let me get you some water and some painkillers for the headache you will no doubt have tomorrow. Don't fall asleep, Jace." He raises his hand in a gesture to tell me okay, but I know he will be out like a light soon, and there is no waking Jace once he has had alcohol and fallen asleep.

I rush to the kitchen and fill up a glass of cold water and grab two painkillers. I don't know when it happened but the night took a turn and the boys got a bit out of control. Jace drank the champagne—which he usually *doesn't* drink—along with Cash. I lost count of the tequila shots they had between them and then they ended the night with a glass of whiskey. No wonder he feels sick, the mixes he had today are lethal. I head back to the bedroom, and Jace is rolling around, trying to get his shoes off. "Here, sit up for me. I'll take your shoes off, you take these and drink the water."

He sits up slowly, holding himself up so he doesn't roll sideways. I pass him the water and tablets, feeling like I'm passing a glass full of water to a one-year-old who just started walking. I hover my hand near the glass as he takes a sip and then throws the pills in his mouth and takes another sip. He gives me the glass back and I place it on the bedside table.

"What would I do without you, Ry Bear," he mumbles.

I smile to myself and bend down to take his shoes off, he doesn't call me Ry Bear a lot but it's cute when he does. He says I give cuddles like a big cuddly bear and he thinks bears are cute, so he says they remind him of me.

Once I have his shoes off, he's staring at me with glazed, bloodshot eyes. I place my hands on his knees and smile at him.

"You feeling okay, babe?"

"I'm seeing three of you right now, but I'm not complaining," he says with what I can only assume is an attempt at a wink but ends up blinking both eyes at me.

I gasp. "Three!? You could never handle three of me, Jace."

"Don't I know it," he mumbles while lying back in bed. I undo his pants, but he keeps kicking his feet.

"Stay still, I need to get you undressed."

I get his trousers off, but I struggle with his top, so I leave it on. It won't hurt him wearing it, and he can always take it off during the night if he gets too hot.

I move his leg to the side so he is lying straight and pull the covers over him. I lie there for a minute and admire him, running my fingers through his slightly tousled hair. He really is my everything, I don't know where I'd be without him these last couple of years. He has been my lifeline. I smile, thinking back to when we first met, our night in Freedom. It's ironic that six years later roles are reversed and I'm sitting here helping him while he is drunk. Although, I have been here more than once.

I still find it insane he wanted to see me again after that night. I remember the day he dropped me home and I assumed it would be the last time I saw him, but he told me it wouldn't be. I remember those butterflies I felt and the excitement. I remember going back into my apartment and Toni bombarding me with questions but not even speaking because I was still on cloud nine because he wanted to see me again. That cloud slowly floated down to hell when I thought of the state I must have been in and the vomit he had to clean up.

However, I was back on cloud nine when my phone rang the following night and it read *Jace*. I'd had no idea how he got my number or how his got programmed into my phone. He had told me on the phone he did it himself while I was asleep. I wasn't mad about that; I was so happy he had called me. A few days later, we were sitting at a table in a gorgeous restaurant called Imperials, which is now our favorite and we visit frequently, giggling and flirting. I had the most amazing night. He was an utter gentleman and didn't even come up to my apartment when he brought me home in a taxi. He called me the following morning, asking if I wanted to go for a walk and coffee around Rose Gardens in Baltimore. The rest is history.

Here we are today, and I have never been happier. I lucked out that night. Toni is adamant it's all thanks to her, I partially agree. If it wasn't for her begging and nonstop nagging to go out, I wouldn't have, then I wouldn't have met the love of my life. Cheesy, I know, but he is. We have our bickers like any couple, but after a while it's forgotten about, we say sorry, kiss, and make up, and it's like it never happened. I truly couldn't ask for anyone better. I lean forward, planting a kiss on his head, and whisper, "I love you, Jace Stiles."

****

I wake up at 9:00 a.m. the next morning and roll over, and Jace is still asleep. I know exactly what he will need when he wakes up with a horrible hangover, and that is his favorite: pancakes and crispy maple bacon covered in maple syrup. I creep out of bed, throwing my robe on, and head to the kitchen. I prepare the breakfast and make him a black coffee with one sugar, just the way he likes it. I then make him an ice-cold glass of water because water never tastes so good when you are hungover with a dry mouth. The next morning's dry mouth can be hell.

I walk back to the bedroom, and Jace is slightly sat up, resting his head against the headboard, looking at me lazily, but his eyes light up as soon as he sees what I'm carrying. "Ya know, your eyes should light up like that for me, not the food," I tease while walking over to him. He scoots up the headboard and smiles up at me as I place the food tray on his lap.

"You know you're always my light, Ry, there is no light brighter than you." He smiles at me, then ruins the moment. "However, food is a different story when I'm feeling like this." He rubs his hands together, looking down at the food. I roll my eyes with a smirk and lie next to him.

I pick up the remote, turning the TV on while he eats his food. I flick through the channels, not much is on but then I come across *Friends*. I have seen every episode a handful of times, but every time I watch it, it still feels like the first time. I sip my coffee and drink my vanilla protein shake. Most days, I drink a shake for breakfast. I indulge sometimes but my weight is very yo-yo so I have to, unfortunately, keep an eye on what I eat. Not that Jace is bothered, but I am conscious of it, so I like to try stay at a weight I'm happy with. Jace is hoovering the food into his mouth like it's about to escape, and I'm trying to work out if he's breathing while demolishing what is on the plate.

"Nice," I say, raising an eyebrow. He just nods while shoveling more pancake into his mouth while the syrup drips down his chin. I let him finish because I will not get much conversation out of him while he eats. He finishes, then places the tray on the floor beside him.

"Thanks for that, beautiful," he says, picking up his coffee.

I flick my eyes to him. "Did you have a good night last night?"

"Yeah, what I remember. The last part of the night is a bit of a blur." He rubs his hand down his face.

"Mmm, I'm sure it is." I take a sip of my shake and slide my eyes back to the TV.

"Your dad seemed to have a good time, he's definitely happier." I want to know if Cash said anything about Becky, like how serious it was. Jace is always up for gossiping with me, but we have never gossiped about his dad, so I'm trying to skirt around it and hope he spills the beans. Who am I kidding, I'll just outright ask if he doesn't.

"Yeah, it has to be Becky." He shrugs. *Why can't men be more like women and be dying to tell us every detail.*

"Did he say anything," I say while keeping my eyes on the TV.

He shakes his head, taking another sip of his coffee while watching *Friends*. "No, he didn't even mention her to me and Boh at work. You know what my dad's like."

"Moody prick? Oh, yeah, I know," I tease.

Jace laughs. "I don't know, there was a difference to him last night. He's normally too uptight out of work. He always wants to be in the office, working nonstop, anything outside of work is . . ."

"Unimportant? Irrelevant? Annoying?" I add in.

"I wouldn't put it like that, he just loves what he does, and when he's away from it, he's uncomfortable, I guess." He shrugs. "He doesn't like being away from his work and letting go or having fun. A bit like me with you," he says, leaning over and placing a kiss on my temple.

I turn to him, raising an eyebrow. "How is your dad's work obsession like you and me?"

"Not obsession," Jace states, still watching *Friends*. "More like a security blanket," he says with another shrug. He looks at me as

I wait for him to continue. "My dad's work is his security blanket and you're mine. I never feel fully myself when I'm not with you."

My stomach flips. The way he can say things so casually but have no idea the effect they have on me.

I lean over, planting a big kiss to his lips.

"I love you, Mr. Stiles," I murmur into his lips.

"Always?" He smiles.

"Forever," I state while lying back against the headboard so he can finish his coffee.

"We should talk more about the vacation you promised me." I smile at him.

"We can look at some places tonight if you want, babe." Jace stands and picks his empty tray up off the floor.

I get up and grab the tray from him.

"Yeah, that sounds good. Remember, I'm brunching with Toni today, but I'll be home by about six, so we can have a look then?"

"Sounds good, baby. Thank you for breakfast, it was nearly as amazing as you." He winks and slaps my ass as he heads into our en suite.

I roll my eyes while walking out of the room but shout over my shoulder for him to not take long. Our main bathroom only has a bath, but I don't fancy one of those today, I would rather have a shower.

"You could always join me," he shouts back through the closed door.

I stare at the bathroom door. "Fuck it." I place the tray on the bed and walk straight into the bathroom.

Chapter 4

The city is busy today, there is some kind of market going on near the seaport—according to the Uber driver—causing an annoying amount of traffic. We are basically gridlocked, it doesn't seem like we're going to move. I will be so late if I stay here, and we might lose our reservation.

"Excuse me, can I just jump out here?" He nods. I jump out, spin around, and tell him "Thank you" before slamming the door. I'm only about a ten-minute walk. I glimpse at the time, and it's five minutes to noon. I will be slightly late but hopefully, Toni is there.

Luckily, I'm wearing thigh-high flat boots and not heels. I kept it casual with jeans and a button-up top. I pinned my hair up in a tight bun on the top of my head. It was greasy and I couldn't be bothered to wash it this morning. The shower Jace and I took, took far too long, which had me rushing to get ready.

Blossoms comes into view as I round the corner. This place is Toni's and my favorite place to have bottomless brunch. It also lights up the whole high street. It's neon-pink sign that says *Blossoms* can be seen from half a mile away. The whole shop front is surrounded by all kinds of pink flowers. It's truly stunning and grabs your attention when you walk past. It's one of the most popular bars in Baltimore. They only started doing bottomless brunch a couple of years back.

This is our weakness, we love a bottomless brunch, and we tested it out and the food was amazing, also the fact they're one of the only places in Baltimore that does bottomless brunch for not one but two hours with unlimited cocktails. A lot of the places we have been to in the past, only do a certain prosecco or wine with a selection of beers. We love cocktails so this was a win, win for us. I haven't seen Ton since my birthday a month ago, so this catch-up is well overdue, and Toni always has the best gossip, and sometimes a lunch and goss with your bestie is all you need.

I walk into Blossoms, trying to control my breathing and not make it obvious how unfit I am from that speed walk. I let the girl know at the reservations stand I have a table under Rylee, and she tells me to go through as my friend is already here. I scan the open area, which has a few empty tables, and then I see big autumn-brown eyes staring straight back at me, and she's wearing a huge grin that reaches her eyes.

I squeal on the spot, walking quickly to the table. As I approach, Toni stands. She's stunning in a pair of black tights, beige Ugg boots, and a beige jumper dress.

"Ahhh!" Toni grabs me in the biggest hug. I have missed her so much. I pull her tighter into me, hugging her like I haven't seen her in years. It feels like that sometimes. She buries her face into my hair before pulling away and grabbing my face with both hands.

"I missed you so fucking much, Ry."

"I missed you so much too, Ton." I take a seat, and she sits opposite me at our two-seater table.

"So how has my beautiful girl been?" She smiles while picking up the menu and going straight to the cocktail section.

"I've been good, you know, the usual, working, more working, and Jace." I laugh. Toni is smiling down at the menu, probably struggling with what five cocktails she wants.

"How have you been?" I ask warily. I know she had trouble with a man a while ago, he wanted to commit and settle down. She didn't. So she called it off with him, but I know she did like him and that's a big thing for Toni.

"Yeah, not bad, thank you. Just working a lot." She looks at me with a smile that doesn't quite reach her eyes.

She changes the conversation quickly, asking if I have picked my cocktail. I will press, but I also know she wants us to catch up on all the goss and not her love life, so I push it aside for now, making a mental note to speak to her about this later. I don't want her holding back from me. She has been there for me through so much, and I want to make sure she knows I'm here to do the same.

"You know already what I'm going for," I say with a sly smile.

"Pornstar Martini, am I right?"

"Got it in one," I say, laughing. "Let me guess, you are going for the Bahama Mama?"

"Always, you know how much I love my Malibu, baby."

The waiter walks over, and we tell them we are having the bottomless brunch, they take our food order to which we have the same, chicken burger with chips and coleslaw. Toni is my soulmate, we love all the exact same things, except Malibu because that is just awful. *Weirdo.*

"So, spill, I want to know everything that I have missed out on since I last saw you, down to what you had for dinner each night," I say in a serious tone, knowing Toni will take the sarcasm from it.

Before Toni can start, she glares over my right shoulder, and her shoulders tense.

I frown and turn around. James Sinclair. Jace's old best friend.

"I swear, why is he always around, he's such a creep," she hisses, still looking at him. I turn back around to her.

"A creep you fucked, let's just remind you of that," I say, smirking at her with a raised eyebrow.

"God, don't remind me." She shudders and points in my face. "We said we would never mention that again."

I put my hands in the air. "Sorry, just had to remind you." I laugh.

She mutters "Bitch," but then she tenses up again as she looks behind me.

"Ladies."

I plaster on a smile and turn around again.

"James," I say, standing, opening my arms to hug him. "Fancy seeing you here."

"Yes, such a shock," Toni says sarcastically. If James hears Toni, he doesn't react, or he just doesn't realize her sarcasm. He hugs me back, squeezing me tight and hugging me for a few seconds too long like he normally does. I step back and take my seat. I take James in, and he hasn't changed much since the first night I met him at Freedom. Just smarter-looking, I guess. He is always in suits, as he is a lawyer, so he's always immaculately dressed.

He gives Toni an awkward wave, she gives him a barely there smile, which blankets us with awkward tension.

"What brings you here today?" I ask, hoping it breaks some of the tension.

He scratches the back of his head and throws his thumb over his shoulder, bringing my attention to the bar where a beautiful brunette stands, sipping on a glass of prosecco.

"I'm on a date. I heard this place was nice. Jace mentioned it a while back actually, and funnily enough, said how much you loved it, so I thought it would be a good place to bring a first date."

It must have been a while ago, as Jace and James are not as close as they used to be. Jace said he changed and became a bit distant and snappy toward him. I see him around town, a lot. The last few times I have seen him, he's appeared tired and worn out. The black circles under his eyes get more pronounced each time. He has lost some weight as well. I suppose it could be the job, but I may mention this to Jace.

I snap my attention back to James. "Oh, that is great, James." I beam at him. His shoulders stiffen, and he gives me a pinched smile with a sour expression.

Weird.

"Yeah, well, I best be going, I don't want to keep her waiting. I just thought I would pop over and say hi," he says with a hard edge to his voice.

"No, you wouldn't. Goodbye, have a nice date," Toni says. I wince, but James just bends down and kisses my cheek and walks away.

He walks back to the bar and then I turn around to Toni.

"You're a fucking nightmare sometimes, you didn't have to make it so obvious that you don't like him. Furthermore, I always seem to forget, why is it that you don't actually like him again?" I scowl at her.

"He just gives me the creeps in general, there is something not quite right about him, Ry. I can't pinpoint what it is, but I always listen to my gut, and he has red flags surrounding him," she warns, furrowing her brows. "And no, not the good red flags either, the bad ones."

"There're good and bad red flags? Huh? Never knew that," I mutter, rolling my eyes.

"You wouldn't." She smirks, her face softening "You're walking around owning the biggest green one there is."

"I'll take that, I love my green flag."

"You should, he's perfect," Toni adds. "Furthermore"—she raises her finger—"I recall you telling me you got a creepy vibe off him the day you returned from Jace's after that night and after me telling you I had done you know what with him." She raises her eyebrows at that as she can't even bring herself to say *fuck him*. She is right though, I said that.

"I know, I know. I used to, but when I got to know him through Jace, he grew on me, and I realized he was just very friendly."

"My next door neighbor, Marilyn, is friendly, that"—she points over my shoulder at, I'm assuming, James—"is darn right creepy."

Before I can say anything else, the waiter arrives at the table, placing down our drinks. James leaves our minds the minute the cocktails are placed in front of us. As soon as she has turned around, Toni and I dive for our drinks, but before we can take a sip, we raise our glasses and cheers.

"To the baddest bitches ever."

"Here, here," I say, clinking my glass with hers. We moan out at the same time, nothing hits like a cocktail, especially when it's in the company of your best friend.

Chapter 5

"You are not going to believe what I have to tell you about what happened at work the other day." Toni beams, wide-eyed, grabbing my hand placed on the table in front of her.

She always has some goss from work to tell me. She works as a recruitment consultant with large corporate companies in the city. This woman could talk her way out of a paper bag, so it's the perfect role for her.

Apparently, it came out that there was a huge affair going on with two of her colleagues, and one of the wives turned up at the office going apeshit and smashed his car up outside in the parking lot. She also punched the girl he was having an affair with.

I have never known someone to always have a story to tell, but Toni sees and hears it all. She's not one of those typical gossips, she literally holds it all in and then tells me as soon as she sees me.

Toni fills me in on a guy she met on a dating site she has seen a few times. I love how free-spirited this girl is and there is no shame, as there shouldn't be. She is still young, enjoying her life, and will eventually meet someone she knows is the one. Until then, she is doing her, and I love her so much for it.

Neither of us realize we have been talking away and that two hours has passed. We have eaten our food and drank a good handful of cocktails. I get my phone out to order the Uber, as does Toni. She lives in the opposite direction, so it makes no sense getting the same one. Mine says it will be ten minutes, Toni's will be here in a few.

We stand up and put our jackets on, and she sways a bit. We giggle as we head to the door. Toni has always been a lightweight. We walk past James and his date as we are leaving, and they seem like they are getting ready to leave too. I give them a small wave, and the girl smiles brightly at me, waving back. I'm sure James explained who we are.

Toni bumps my shoulder and says, "Don't say I'm being silly . . ." She side-eyes me. "But don't you think she resembles you a bit, Ry?"

Confused, I look at Ton. "Who?"

"James's date."

I laugh. "You really have drank too much. No, she doesn't. There're loads of brunettes around," I say, raising my hand to gesture to girls walking passed us with long brunette hair.

"Mmm, true, maybe it is the alcohol." She laughs. "Damn. My Uber got here quick," she pouts, pointing to a car pulling up.

I stick my bottom lip out. "I hate adulting," I say as I pull her in for the biggest hug, knowing it will probably be a month or even two before I see her next. Between her and me working and other plans, we don't always get to see each other as much as we'd like. People find it funny because we voice note on WhatsApp everyday, but it's not the same as seeing someone in person.

"I know, but I had the best time with you, Ry. I missed you so fucking much," she says, giving me an extra squeeze. She pulls away and gives me a big sloppy kiss on my cheek.

"You will go back in there"—she points to the entrance door to Blossoms—"and wait there until your Uber comes, won't you?" She backs away from me and bumps into someone. We both let out a giggle while raising our hands and apologizing to the person who huffs and walks off.

"Get home safe," I say.

"Please message me once you're home," she shouts as she gets to the back passenger door.

I raise my hand and blow her a kiss, and she catches it and puts it in her pocket. This is something we have done since we were kids. We always used to "save our kisses for when we really needed them," but we never grew out of it. Now if we're on the phone talking and one of us is down in the dumps, we will remind each other to grab a kiss from our pocket and slap it on our cheek. It always cheers us up. I wave to her as the Uber drives away.

My phone pings twenty seconds later with a message from her telling me to go wait inside. She knows me too well, as I'm still standing outside waiting. I ignore her message because the tracker says it will be here in a few minutes.

I hear giggling and turn around to James helping his date into her coat, and I smile to myself. It's nice to see him with someone.

Yes, Toni thinks he's creepy, and I can see why she would think that, but behind it all, he's very friendly and has had bad luck with women in the past. Me being his friend's girlfriend, he just feels comfortable with me, and I'm fine with that. He has never done anything to make me think any less of him.

James catches me staring and smiles wide at me.

"You waiting for Jace?" he asks.

"Oh, no, he's working today, my Uber is going to be here any minute."

"Oh, no, don't worry about an Uber, I'm driving, I can take you home." I look at him and then his date, she is standing there smiling at me, unbothered, but I don't want to intrude, they may have been going somewhere.

"That is really lovely of you, James, but I don't want to intrude, you carry on having a nice day."

Before James can reply, his date jumps in. "Oh no, I have work now which is just down the road, James is dropping me."

"Okay, if you're sure, James?" I ask, shrugging.

He brushes me off. "Of course, Ry, don't be silly."

I pull my phone out, canceling my Uber, and follow them to his car.

When we arrive at the car, his date spins around and pushes her hand out to me. "I'm Casey, by the way."

"It's lovely to meet you, I'm Rylee." I beam at her.

"Yes, James told me about you, and ahhh," she says, squinting.

"Jace?" I slip in.

"Yes, sorry, James mentioned you were his friend's girlfriend, I just couldn't remember his friend's name," she says, hitting her forehead.

I laugh it off while we get in the car.

She literally works around the corner, and we move for all of about forty seconds before she is directing him to pull over outside a club. I have never been here before, but it's decent from the outside. I sit there, gazing out the window, not sure if they will say goodbye inside the car or get out. Thankfully, James steps out of the car, and Casey spins around from the front seat and says her goodbyes. I tell her it was lovely to meet her, and I hope to see her again soon. She seems like a lovely girl. Hopefully, James will go on another date with her. I have always wanted to double date, but Jace's friends are absolute manwhores, so it's hard.

James gets back in the car a minute later.

"Are you not going to get in the front?" He looks at me with an eyebrow raised.

"Oh, of course, I was in my own little world back here." I get out of the car and slip into the front seat.

James pulls away. It's silent but a comfortable silence.

"So how was your lunch with Toni?"

"It was nice, thank you. It's always good to catch up with her. I miss her a lot. You know what it's like being an adult now with responsibilities, we don't always get to see each other."

He nods along.

"How was your date? You, of course, don't have to tell me," I rush out. I don't want him thinking I'm being nosey. I so am, but I don't want him thinking that.

He chuckles. "It went well . . . I think. She seemed really nice, easy to talk with and really interesting. She wants to meet up again, so that's a good sign, right?"

It makes me smile that he's asking me for advice and trusts me enough to speak about this.

"Of course it is. She would be crazy to not want to meet up with you again."

His smile drops, and he glimpses at me, then at the road and then at me again. *What did I say wrong?*

"Wha-what, really, you think that?" He tilts his head.

"Erm, yes, you're a great person, James," I say, not knowing if I have said something wrong.

His face lights up as if he just won the lottery. He nods to himself, and I'm sure I see him puff his chest out slightly. Okay . . . maybe he needed a little confidence boost. Everyone needs them sometimes.

We drive the rest of the journey in silence, although there is a slight awkwardness in the air.

We pull up to mine and Jace's apartment. I grab my bag and turn to James, giving him a quick peck on the cheek.

"Thank you so much for driving me home, James. I really appreciate it."

"Of course, Rylee, I couldn't see you getting an Uber."

I give him a smile and step out of the car.

"See you later, James," I say as I gently close his car door. I walk up the path and key in the code to enter the building. As I walk in and turn around to close the glass doors, I realize he is still sitting in the car watching me . . . with a huge smile on his face. I give him another wave in the hopes this will send him on his way. He returns my wave but doesn't move. I head up to my apartment, and once I'm inside, I tiptoe to the window and peek through a crack in the blinds. He has now gone. *Okay, Toni may be right, a little creepy.*

Chapter 6

I open my eyes to darkness and am a bit disorientated, then realize I'm lying on our sofa. I must have fallen asleep. *God, what time is it?* I hunt around for my phone, which I find on the floor next to the sofa. I light up the screen, squinting at the brightness, and see it's 7:00 p.m.

"Fuck," I mutter while rubbing my eyes. I then see a text from Jace.

> Jace: Hey beautiful, I'm heading to the pub with Rowan after work so I'll be home a bit later. Don't worry about making me any food, I'll get something at the pub.

That was only sent half hour ago, so I type out a text back.

> Me: Okay babe, have a good night and be safe. Xo

Rowan is Jace's best friend, they have been best friends since they were kids. They are workaholics, so they don't get to see each other as much as they would like. Rowan does sometimes pop around if he's in the area. He is a contractor and sometimes has work sites around here. I have gotten along with him since the first time I met him. Well, second. However, the first time, I don't remember much. He was with Jace that night at Freedom. Apparently, we talked when we were at the tables, but it's pretty much a blank night for me.

As it's just me tonight, so I think I will binge eat some junk food and stick a film on from Netflix. I'm still full from our brunch earlier and don't fancy a dinner. I walk over to the cupboard, grabbing a big bag of chips and some chocolate out of the fridge, because chocolate belongs in the fridge. I put chips in a big bowl and walk over to the couch, placing the chips and chocolate on the coffee table.

I can't sit and get comfy in my clothes, I have to be in pj's. I head to my bedroom to go put some on with an added spring in my step when I think about my night. I love being with Jace but a night on your own to eat what you want and watch what you want is underrated. Once I have my comfiest and most unflattering pj's on, I walk out of my bedroom and head to the sofa to turn the TV on.

I flop myself down on the sofa and pull the blanket over my legs to get myself comfy. I flick through Netflix but can't find anything that screams "watch me." So I flick through Amazon Prime to see if there are any good films but, again, I find nothing. I then remember a film I watched a few months back called *The In Between* on Netflix, it was one of the most emotional films I have ever watched and because I'm a masochist and love torturing myself, I'm going to watch it again.

I load it up and my eyes fill with tears just looking at the cover of the film. The film is about a girl who meets a guy at a cinema. They are the only two people watching the film, but the girl doesn't realize the film is in Italian, and the boy—very cute, might I add—sits next to her and offers to translate the film. It's very romantic and super sweet. They leave after without exchanging numbers or anything. She crosses paths with him again and it goes from there. Something traumatizing happens and he passes away, and it is gut-wrenching, but he tries to communicate with her from the other side, and they meet in this place called "the in between."

It is emotional, and I honestly can't remember the last time I ugly cried that hard. Jace was doing some work for his dad at the time in his study, and when he came out, he thought someone in my family had died. I could barely breathe.

So, here we are. Ready to do this all over again. I honestly have no idea why I do this to myself. A glass of wine might help.

I jump up and head into the kitchen to pour myself a glass of my favorite sauvignon blanc. Although, I love the film, I'm nervous before even watching it because I know what state I will be in afterward. I head back to the couch and take a seat, getting comfy again. I brought the bottle of wine with me—I think I will need it.

By the end of the film, the food has been demolished, the bottle of wine is empty, and I also have gone through nearly a roll of toilet paper from crying so much. *How could someone go through losing the person they love at such a young age?* I couldn't imagine losing Jace. I know that may sound cringey, but losing someone is hard enough if they break up with you, or vice versa, but losing someone in such a tragic way, I don't think I could ever get over it. It makes me miss Jace, and I just want to hug him.

It's only 10:00 p.m. I doubt he will be home soon. I think it's best I go to bed. I love the film so much, but God, it makes me depressed! I head upstairs and brush my teeth, and while I'm brushing my teeth, I check my phone to see if there is a text from Jace saying if he is on his way home. He sometimes texts me to say when he is on his way back, but other times, he doesn't. I don't mind so much as I am the world's worst at remembering to text him when I'm out.

Unfortunately, there is no text, and all that crying has made me so tired. I think I'll be asleep in no time. I finish in the bathroom and walk to our joint closet. I pull one of Jace's tops out and take off my pj's. I want to smell him before going to sleep, and I hate sleeping in a full set of pj's. I get under the covers and snuggle up into my pillow. I really can't wait to see Jace and just touch him and tell him I love him. *Never take someone for granted because you don't know how long you may have left with them.*

Chapter 7

A warmth comes over me, and an arm curls tightly around my waist. I smell him before I even open my eyes and turn around. He smells fresh—he knows to have a shower before getting into bed with me, there is no way I am waking up to the smell of beer. I turn around and squint at the lamp he has turned on.

"Shit, sorry, baby, I didn't think you would wake up. I was just about to turn it off."

I smile. It feels so nice to be looking at him and his beautiful face.

"It's okay. I'm just glad you're home, I missed you."

A frown appears on his face as he brings his hand up to cup my jaw so he can see my face better.

"Ry, what's happened, are you okay? Your eyes are so swollen."

I let out a small laugh.

"I'm fine, I stupidly watched that film I watched a few months ago that had me bawling. This time you weren't here to hug me though," I pout.

Jace takes his hand from my jaw and slides his arm under my shoulders while pulling me into him. "Aww, my baby. Why did you watch that film when it makes you upset?" he says while kissing my forehead.

I shrug, men don't understand. A lot of women love watching films that upset them. I have no idea why, but we do. It's like *Titanic*, it makes me cry every single time, but I still love watching it.

"Well, I'm here now. You know you could have text me."

"I know, but you were out, and it was my fault for watching the film anyway."

"Well, I don't care. You know you can always text me if you're upset." *How lucky can I get?* I purposely watched a film I knew would upset me and if I had text him telling him that, he would have left his friends and come home, even though I brought it on myself.

"I know you don't care, Jace, that's why I love you. I'm glad you woke me up, even if it was by accident," I say before kissing the tip of his nose.

Before I can lie my head back down on his chest, he cups my face with his hand and brings himself lower and gently kisses my lips. He pulls back a little, eyes locked on my mouth, and then brings his lips to mine again and kisses me more forcefully, and he runs his tongue along my bottom lip, so I open my mouth wider. Jace slips his tongue in, and my tongue tangles with his, the kiss turning more frantic as the seconds goes by. He takes his arm from behind me and grabs my face, holding me with both hands while my head falls to the pillow. Jace moves so he is leaning over me and carries on kissing me. Moving down my neck, he adds suction to his kisses. I'm breathing heavily, trying to rub my legs together to get relief, but Jace has most of his weight pinning me down.

"Jace, I need you, please," I pant while running my hands up his back and digging my nails in to show my frustration and need for him. The slickness between my legs is growing.

While moving lower on my body, Jace plants an open-mouthed kiss over my left nipple and sucks lightly. I lull my head back, moaning. He adds another kiss on my belly.

"So . . ." he whispers, moving down farther.

"Fucking . . ." He places another kiss on my pubic bone.

I make eye contact with him, and he's staring straight at me with pure heat flaming his eyes.

"Jace, please."

Jace blows a small bit of air on my throbbing clit, which makes me moan.

"Sexy."

Before I can scream at him, he places his mouth over my clit and sucks hard, and my back arches off the bed, and I swear I see stars. My pussy is pulsating as Jace eats me like I'm his last meal. His eyes are closed and he's humming like it's the most delicious thing he has ever tasted. Him enjoying this just increases the sensation flowing through me.

Jace rubs gentle circles on my clit while fucking me with his tongue. He pulls his tongue out of my entrance and replaces it with two thick fingers and then brings his tongue to my clit. I'm in actual heaven, I don't want him to ever stop. He finger-fucks me deep and fast while keeping suction on my clit, and my eyes roll back in my head as I run my fingers through his hair and tug on it while keeping him where he is. I moan as the orgasm builds in the pit of my stomach.

"Jace, I'm coming, fuck, please don't stop."

Jace fucks me relentlessly with his fingers and grazes his teeth against my clit, which causes my undoing. My orgasm hits me hard—the euphoria flowing through my body—Jace is still pumping his fingers in and out of me slowly, prolonging the feeling. I open my eyes as I come down from my orgasm, and I feel like I'm floating on clouds as I come back to earth. Jace has pure lust in his eyes, and I smile lazily at him while letting go of the death grip I have on his hair.

I shut my eyes and sigh, my body relaxing and feeling the best it's ever felt. Jace pulls his fingers out of me as I look at him, then his fingers, and they are covered in my juices. He spreads his fingers, the juices stringing from one to the other, and puts one finger in his mouth while closing his eyes and humming. Then he pulls it out.

"You don't understand how fucking good you taste, Ry. I think you need to taste yourself to know just how good it is."

He brings his second finger to my mouth, and I open wide for him, keeping eye contact the whole time. I close my lips around his finger and suck, and it's surprisingly pleasant and sweet. I close my eyes while sucking his finger like I would his dick. Jace groans and yanks his finger out of my mouth and then pulls down his boxers.

He grabs me by my thighs and pulls me down the bed like I weigh nothing and positions my legs over his broad shoulders.

Jace's eyes are filled with pure hunger. Hunger for me.

"You don't know what you do to me, Ry," he says as he slams into me with brutal force, not even giving me a minute to adjust. He pulls back out and slams into me again. My head falls back as I scream out. It feels like he's hitting my cervix with every slam, and he doesn't let up.

"Jace, fuck," I scream.

"Fuck, Fuck, Fuckkkkk. Your greedy pussy is squeezing me so fucking tight," he rasps out while looking down at where he's pounding into me. All I hear above my moans and Jace's heavy breathing is the slickness as he thrusts in and out of me. The wetness runs down to my asshole and soaks the mattress. Jace keeps up the force, pushing my legs back so my hips rise as he leans into me more. I didn't think he could get any deeper, but in this position, it borderline hurts, but there is no way I want him to stop. His eyes meet mine as he speeds up.

"Rylee," Jace says painfully. "Baby, I need you to come." He pinches my clit which causes my back to raise off the bed.

"Ahhhh," I shout.

"Your greedy pussy needs filling with my cum baby. Come! Now!" he grits out while applying more pressure to my clit. I let go and allow the wave take me, and I pulse around his cock. He grunts and slams himself into me before he stills.

"Mmmm" is all I hear from him as he collapses on top of me, heat radiating from his body. His heart is jackhammering against my chest along with mine. We are breathing heavily, basking in post orgasmic bliss. I run my fingers through his hair, massaging his scalp. He sits up, pulling out, which makes me wince. I'm sore but in a good way. He smiles at me and kisses my forehead.

I get up, heading to the bathroom to clean myself up. I sit on the toilet for a while, it stings a lot. Jace doesn't always fuck me like that, but I can't say I hate it, I love it, it's like a raw act of possession breaks out of him. Once I have peed and cleaned myself up, I tiptoe back to our bed, and Jace is in bed waiting for me. His lazy eyes take me in, running the length of my body, and I blush. He still makes me feel like a giggly little girl when he shows me attention. I slide in next to him, cuddling up to his side, my head resting on his chest listening to his now-calm heartbeat.

"You're so perfect. Night, babe," he murmurs into my hair.

I smile to myself, closing my eyes.

"Night, Jace."

Chapter 8

The following morning, I wake up sweating. Jace is squished up against me with his arm and legs thrown over me. I love having him this close, but I hate being hot. I throw his arm off me and try to kick his leg which, of course, does not make him budge even an inch. The next thing I know, his arm is slung back around me. *Nope, I can't have this.*

"Jace," I say while shaking him slightly.

"Mmm," he says, hugging me tighter.

"Can you let go of me, I'm literally dripping with sweat and so are you. I need to get up and shower."

"Sorry, baby," he murmurs.

He rolls away from me so I can get up. I look over at his bedside table and see he didn't bring a bottle of water to bed with him, so I pop into the kitchen to grab him one and place it on his bedside table.

I jump in the shower and stand under the steaming hot water. My body aches today but in the best way. I finish in the shower and head into the bedroom. Jace is sitting up on his phone with a deep scowl on his face, like he's reading something in depth.

"Morning . . . you okay?"

He sighs, then smiles.

"I am now," he says and lies back down. "Come give me a hug."

I skip over to him, still in my towel. I tighten it around me. He opens his legs so I can lie between them. I lie on my stomach so my head is laying on his stomach. He rests one hand around the top of my back and the other playing with my hair because he knows that's my favorite.

He sits there in silence, and I know something is up.

"What's up?" I murmur, staring out at the gray clouds through our bedroom window.

He sighs. "Just work, we have taken on this huge new project for this company, and it's just taking up a lot of my time and my energy. Dad is being moody because it's a big deal and he wants it to go smoothly." I roll my eyes. His dad is always fucking moody, this is no shock to me.

"What is it? Is your dad putting pressure on you? Surely, being his son, you can tell him to back off a bit?"

"Nah, that's the thing, Dad is trying to take the workload from me to him, but it's putting more stress on him. Which I don't want." He sighs. "He has enough. I'm trying to line up one of the trainers to help take some of the workload off us. It will be a good learning resource for them."

I nod. "So does this mean you got to work today as well, then?" I say, trying not to sound disappointed. I don't want to stress him out any more, but it would be nice to have a day at home with him.

"Nah, I'm all yours today, beautiful. I was just sorting out a couple of emails, but it's all done now."

I move my head, looking up at him, resting my chin on his stomach. "I want us to have a day of doing nothing. Well, I want you to do nothing. I'm going to cook us a nice dinner later tonight. We can just chill on the sofa and watch a film later, does that sound good to you?"

"Sounds perfect." He grins.

I rise to my hands and knees, leaning forward, giving him a kiss. Jace holds the back of my head, keeping me there, and deepens the kiss, his tongue probing at my lips to let him in. I open my mouth, angling my head to the side, tangling my tongue with his. I love kissing him, the fact he is an amazing kisser makes it all that more toe-curling. The kiss turns erratic, teeth clashing. I know this is what he needs to de-stress from work, and I'm more than happy to give it to him. I pull myself away, seeing the desire in his dilated pupils. I know he can see how much I want him.

"Lay back," I whisper.

He lies back, not taking his eyes off me.

I kiss down his neck, taking my time, then kiss down his chest. When I move my lips down more, his hard length is poking out from his boxers, laying over his belly button. Jace is big in length and girth. I remember the first time I saw his dick, and I'm not embarrassed to say I panicked. Although I wasn't a virgin, I hadn't had sex in a while, so the first time with him was nice but it did hurt. He was so gentle with me, and I'm sure he felt me wince when he entered me.

I kiss over the head of his cock, slowly making my way down his length over his boxers.

"Rylee," Jace growls.

I smile into his dick as I'm kissing it, moving to his balls. I won't tease him, as I know he's stressed. Not that he would ever let me tease him.

I pull his boxers down, revealing his beautiful cock. I know they say dicks are ugly, but Jace's is beautiful, long, thick, and veiny. Trust me, before I met Jace, I would have cringed at a girl saying that, but I get it now. I lick up his length and slide my tongue to just under the head of his dick, I know that's a weakness for him. He jerks his hips up, seeking my mouth. I slide my tongue over the slit, opening wide, sliding halfway down.

"Mmm," Jace moans. He grabs the sheet in a tight grip, and I keep going up and down but stopping halfway, adding more spit to his dick, so I can slide him all the way to the back of my throat, making me gag.

"Shit, Ry," Jace hisses out.

I remember to relax my throat and slide my mouth as far down as I can go, taking as much of his dick as I can. I used to think guys hated girls gagging but Jace loves it, he says the softness of my throat closing around the head of his dick feels amazing.

Jace threads his fingers through my hair, gripping my head. "You look so pretty with my cock deep down your throat, baby."

He takes over control, thrusting his hips so his dick hits the back of my throat while also pushing my head down. I gag every time from the force. Saliva mixed with Jace's pre-cum is dripping out of my mouth, pooling over his balls.

"Ahh, stay like that, Rylee, use your hands to touch yourself. I want you coming from your fingers while I come down your throat."

I hum around his dick, sucking like my life depends on it while creating a mess on Jace. I reach down, finding myself wet straight away. The towel has long gone. I gather the juices around my entrance and bring them up to my clit, applying pressure. I am already turned on from sucking Jace's dick, so it's not going to take me long, and as if reading my mind, Jace speeds up, fucking my mouth at a crazed speed.

"Hurry up and get there, Rylee, I can't hold out much longer," he grunts out.

I rub my clit faster, the pressure builds and builds and then I'm screaming around his cock, and the vibrations must send Jace over the edge because the next minute, his salty cum hits the back of my throat. I try to focus on swallowing down his cum while riding out my orgasm. I'm still moaning around his dick, causing some to drip out of my mouth.

Jace twitches in my mouth, quickly pulling me off him by my hair. His heated gaze locks onto my lips.

"You and these lips will be the death of me one day, Ry," he says, rubbing his thumb across my lips, collecting some of his cum still dripping and shoving it in my mouth. I run my tongue around his thumb before he pulls out and grabs my chin, bringing me face-to-face with him, then he leans in and gently kisses me.

"I love you, baby," he whispers.

"Always?"

"Forever."

*****

Jace and I are lying in bed after having a power nap, and he's stroking my hair.

"What film do you want to watch tonight, I'm not doing a sad one," he states, making me laugh.

"No, no sad ones, I promise. I will have a look through Netflix and see what's on."

I then realize I hadn't asked him how his night went.

"Oh, how did your night go? Did you have a good night?"

He shrugs. "Yeah, it was pretty good. It was just me and Rowan but then Danny and James turned up and joined us for a bit."

"How was it with James?" I say while drawing patterns on his chest with the tips of my fingers. He tenses ever so slightly. Every time I mention James since they drifted, Jace acts weird and tries to change the subject. I have pulled him up on it previously, but he just laughs it off and says that it's nothing.

I then remember James's date and want the inner details. Jace knows I love gossiping with him.

I sit up straight, looking at him.

"Did James mention his date?

"Date?" Jace eyes me, eyebrows furrowed.

James not mentioning the date is weird, but I guess if they haven't spoken that much, then I kind of get it, but now I'm thinking he didn't mention seeing me.

"Did James tell you he saw me yesterday at Blossoms and dropped me home?" Jace sits up so quickly it knocks me back a little. "Woah." I put my hands out in front of me.

"What do you mean you saw him and he dropped you home." Jace has turned a shade of red I haven't seen before.

"Erm." I don't even know why I'm struggling to find the words, but I have never seen him like this before. He is glaring at me, waiting for me to finish.

"I was at Blossoms with Toni, and he was there with a date," I rush out. "When he and his date were leaving, he offered me a lift home as he was dropping her back to work."

Jace nods while leaning back on the bed.

"Why didn't James tell you?" I stare at Jace, waiting for him to answer. His chest is rising and falling pretty fast, and he seems pissed off.

"Jace? What has happened?" As if he was in a daydream, he shakes his head and smiles at me.

"Nothing, babe, he must have just forgotten to mention it. I haven't seen or spoken to him in a while, so it just threw me off, that's all."

"Mmm," I say with pursed lips. *Why would he not mention to Jace he had seen me or dropped me home?* The fact he didn't doesn't sit right with me.

"He wasn't out that long, anyway. Dad turned up for a couple of drinks, you know him and Dad don't get along, so James left pretty quickly after that." He shrugs.

Cash hates James. The hate developed right around the same time Jace and James drifted and stopped talking, but even if his name is mentioned, Cash's demeanor changes. This is Cash we are talking about, though; I'm surprised he can stand his own reflection sometimes.

"Speaking of my dad"—he cringes—"I just remembered what he said last night. He's coming around today to help me put up that closet in the spare bedroom. I asked him last night, and he said he would pop around some point this afternoon." *Oh, joys.*

"Jace," I moan at him. "I thought today was going to be our day!" I cross my arms.

"I know, I'm sorry, babe, I promise, tomorrow." He drops his bottom lip out.

I throw my hands up. "Ahhhh. Okay." I look over at the clock on the bedside table and it's just past noon. I best get up and get myself presentable before beloved daddy dearest turns up.

Chapter 9

Jace and Cash have been banging hammers and swearing like there is no tomorrow for the last two hours. Cash turned up at 3:00 p.m. I was hoping he would come earlier so he could go earlier and me and Jace could have the rest of our day to ourselves. I swear to God, he's either working or I am. I don't see him nowhere near as much as I would love to, so days like this are special. However, I have been wanting that closet up for months, so I'm glad it's finally being done.

It's just past five, so I best check on them to see if they want a drink. I walk into the bedroom and stop dead in my tracks. Jace and Cash are topless, and I shamelessly can't even look away. They have a lot of similarities facewise, but my God, even their bodies are similar, although Cash is slightly taller and broader. I keep gawking at them, noting the sweat running down their backs. The window is still shut. It's cold this time of the year, maybe bringing some air in will help. Before I can make them aware of my presence, Jace interrupts my thoughts.

"You good, Ry?" he asks, tilting his head. *Oh my God, where was I looking?* I totally zoned out.

"I, uh, I wanted to see if you both wanted a drink, you have been in here a while," I rush out, scratching my head and trying to act cool. Like I have been caught doing something I shouldn't have. Cash has turned to me, which, for some unknown reason, makes heat flood to my cheeks. For fuck's sake. Jace smirks at me, like he knows.

"A beer, please," Cash mumbles, breaking my attention away from Jace. I nod, turning around and walking back toward the kitchen. Grabbing a beer from the fridge, I realize I didn't ask Jace what he wanted. I'll just get him a beer. I turn around and Jace is standing there with that smirk on his face again. I push the beers out in front of me, motioning for him to take them.

"Cheeks are a bit flushed, you hot?" he teases.

I don't even entertain his wicked attempt at trying to make me more embarrassed.

"No, I'm good, thanks. You can get back to work now." I smile up at him.

"Was you just checking out my dad, Ry?" Jace once again teases.

"Absolutely not," I abruptly state. *Oh, God.* I must have been staring at Cash when Jace saw me. I wasn't even looking at Cash like *that.* I mean, I was but I wasn't. It was more of admiration for like his age, you know?

"Uh-huh." Jace smirks. "He might have the muscles, Ry, but I got more stamina, baby. Remember that." He winks, turning around, walking back to the room, laughing. *Asshole.*

Jace walks into the kitchen, dropping himself on the chair next to me.

"All finished," he says, wiping away the beads of sweat off his head.

I lean up, giving him a kiss on his cheek.

"You're the best." I squeal. I walk to the fridge to get him a beer. I'm so happy those closets are now up. I'm a typical girl who loves shopping and has way too many handbags, shoes, and clothes I will probably never wear again, but you never know. I needed the extra closet space, so Jace said he would build one in my dressing room, which is meant to be a guest room, but I have taken it over with all of my belongings. It took a while, but it's finally done.

"Is your dad still here?" I say before grabbing his beer out the fridge.

"Yeah, he's just packing his tools away. Grab him a beer too, please, babe."

I grab both beers, placing them in front of Jace as Cash walks out.

He grabs the beer off the table and nods as a way of saying thank you. I don't know why the asshole can't just use actual words. I must show him how manners work, clearly.

"Cash," I say, which causes him to stop with his beer midair.

"Thank you for helping Jace with the closet. I really appreciate it," I say, looking him straight in the eye. *I swear to God if he just nods, I will scream.*

"You're welcome, Rylee" is all he says, but it's something. I'll add that to the 300 words he has said to me in the last five years. *Okay, that's an exaggeration, but I bet it's not far off.* He takes a few big gulps of the beer before placing it down on the kitchen side. Jace is on his phone, probably reading emails. *I'm surprised Cash is not doing the same.* As if reading my mind, Cash pulls his phone out of his back pocket, scrolling through it. I'm just standing here like a spare part. I want to see the closet, so I slip away, not that they would notice, heading into my dressing room.

"Ahhhhhh!" I scream.

Feet shuffle down the hall and then Jace and Cash are next to me, glaring at me like I have grown an extra head while I stand here with the biggest grin on my face.

"What? What's wrong?" Jace says.

I grin up at him. "The closet, I just love it so much, look how pretty it is in the room."

I hear what I think is a moody growl next to me from Cash as he exits the room. *Dick.*

I hug Jace around the neck and smack a big kiss on his lips. "Did I tell you how much I love you?"

He pulls a thinking face. "I don't think you have, come to think of it, but you can show me." He winks.

"Later." I smile.

"Now."

I raise my eyebrow at him, realizing he is every bit serious when he says now.

"Your dad is in the next room." I'm now whispering.

"Sooo." Jace smirks, grabbing me by my waist and pulling me in toward him. He kisses up my neck, which gives me goose bumps all over and makes me ache between my legs. A throat clears, and I jump back from Jace. We look toward the door, and Cash is standing there with his hands in his pocket, gazing out the window.

He throws his thumb over his shoulder.

"I'm going to head home," he says with what sounds like annoyance.

"Okay, yeah, thanks for your help today, Dad, I really appreciate it," he says, walking over to his dad.

"No problem." He claps Jace on his back and looks at me.

"Bye, Rylee," he says, his jaw clenched. *What is this guy's deal?*

I'm not rude so I reply, "Bye, Cash. Thanks again for all this"—I wave around at the closet—"I really do appreciate it."

He does his signature nod and walks down the hallway with Jace in tow.

I walk out and Cash is grabbing his coat and heading toward the door. He stops at the door and spins around to Jace.

"Remember what I told you," he says, pointing at Jace. "Make sure you have words."

Jace scratches the back of his head, sliding his eyes to me quickly and then back to his dad, like he has been caught doing something.

I struggle to hold myself back. "Have words with who?"

Cash and Jace look at me, and Cash's shoulders tense and his hands turn white from the grip on the door.

"Could you have not got a taxi?" Cash blurts.

"Dad," Jace hisses, eyes wide.

"Excuse me?" I look at Jace as if to say, *What is he talking about*?

"James" is all Cash says, and he looks straight ahead at nothing.

"Again, excuse me?" I place my hand on my hip, the rage flooding through me. I'm gathering he is talking about James giving me a lift home, but how dare Cash make me feel bad for taking the lift when Jace has never told me what happened between them? In so many words, he basically said they drifted apart.

"Just forget about it, okay," Jace adds. Cash opens the apartment door, but I have to have one last word.

"As I am gathering, you are talking about James giving me a lift home," I blurt out. "I was waiting for an Uber." *Who uses taxis anymore?* "Then he came out with his date and insisted on giving me a lift home. Why wouldn't I say yes? When someone gives me a reason, then we can discuss this."

Cash stares at Jace like he is waiting for him to say something. "Sorry, that was rude of me, Rylee. I'm going." Cash leaves without even a backward glance and doesn't say bye to Jace.

Jace turns to me.

"I'm sorry about that, Ry." Jace seems worn out. I know work is wearing him out and then he did the closet for me today, he doesn't need shit like this going on, so I won't carry anything on.

"Hey, don't worry about it. But I do want to talk about this at some point, okay?" I smile at him.

Jace takes a deep breath and nods.

"How about you go get a shower, you stink," I tease, trying to lighten the mood, which seems to work, as Jace's shoulders drop.

"I will put dinner on and then we sit in front of the TV for the evening and do nothing, how does that sound?" I grin.

He walks over to me, letting out a huge breath.

"You know, Ry Bear, I wonder what I did to deserve you."

"Being you, Jace."

He laughs and then plants a kiss on my forehead before walking toward the bathroom.

While he is in the shower, I prepare dinner. I'm going to cook his favorite tonight, chicken fajitas. As I'm cutting the chicken, I can't help but think something big happened between Jace and James. Jace's reaction to me getting a lift home from James and then Cash's reaction. It's as if they don't want me around him at all. If something bad has happened or something has been said, I need to know. Like I said, I see James a lot. I don't tell Jace every time because sometimes it's simply a "Hey, you okay" as we pass each other on the street or bump into each other in the supermarket. I will wait for Jace to be less pressured at work and then sit down and talk to him about it and find out what happened. It clearly stresses him out. The fact Cash told him to *have words* also doesn't sit right with me.

I jump out of my skin when he speaks. "You seemed deep in thought there, you okay?"

"Yes, of course, just thinking about what film to watch tonight," I lie and carry on cutting up the chicken.

"I will go pick a film, no sad ones," he reminds me.

I laugh and nod. "Okay. Deal."

Chapter 10

Jace and I are cuddled up on the sofa after eating our fajitas, watching his favorite film, *Avengers: Endgame*. He is a huge Marvel geek. He made me watch all the films over two weeks, and I honestly wanted to cry, but he always sits through my films, so I couldn't say no. I don't mind some of them, but a few are boring. I don't dare say that to Jace, he is literally obsessed. His favorite is *Thor*; he said if he could ever be a superhero, it would be him. I always tease and say, *Why? Because you can get a time out to eat like shit and drink beer?* I slyly know that's the reason he would be.

I bought Jace Thor's hammer one year for his birthday. It cost me an arm and a leg but to see his face was worth every penny. He gave the saying "like a kid at Christmas" a new meaning that day because I honestly don't think I have ever seen him so happy. His face soon dropped when I called it a hammer. He said, "*It's a Mjölnir, Rylee. Nothing like a hammer.*" It's like a large version of one. Anyway, he has it on display in his office, along with loads of other Marvel memorabilia he has collected over the years.

I still can't stop thinking about earlier, a part of me is dying to say something too, but I know I'm probably being silly. I hate ignoring that sick feeling in my stomach like something is going to happen and you can't pinpoint what.

I lie between Jace's legs while he is stretched out on the sofa. I have my head on his chest, listening to his steady heartbeat. If I'm ever anxious or worried about something, his heartbeat soothes me. It brings me down to earth and makes me realize how perfect my life is with him and that I have nothing to worry about.

"You okay, baby?" Jace asks.

I frown. "Yeah, of course, why?"

He stares at me as if he's trying to think what to say. He strokes my hair again, knowing I love when he does that. He smiles.

"I just know it's the anniversary of your mom's death tomorrow, and I want you to know I'm always here for you."

There's a painful twinge in my heart. I'm not great at dealing with my feelings, and Jace knows this but always wants me to be more open with him. I treat the anniversary of my mom's death like any other day. Once I think about her too much, I get in a deep hole of grief, so I tend to just not think about her. I know it sounds terrible, and friends, including Jace, have told me it's not the best way to cope with my feelings, but it's my way of dealing with them, and I want to keep it that way, so tomorrow will be like any other day. I do, of course, think about her now and then, but I tend to not let myself dwell on it. Losing her was one of the hardest things I have ever gone through, and if it weren't for Jace, I honestly don't know what I would have done.

I was with Jace when I got the call saying she had been taken to the hospital. She caught pneumonia and was really ill. I went straight to the hospital, and I remember walking in the room and seeing her face, she looked awful and could barely speak. She had chronic obstructive pulmonary disease from smoking, so the pneumonia was not helping. The doctor told me it had started to cling to her other organs, along with having a heart murmur, so she was not doing well. They told us she had fluid on the kidneys and lungs and needed it drained. I sat with her and talked about random stuff, and she was laughing along, so I thought she was getting better.

I got a call that night saying she had passed away. The fluid spread rapidly and went to her heart, and they had been prepping her for emergency surgery to drain the fluid, but she didn't make it. I have never felt pain like it. I cried in Jace's arms for weeks. She was more than my mom, she was my best friend. That was three years ago. I mask those feelings now because it hurts like you wouldn't believe, and I can't put myself back there again, and I know my mom wouldn't want me too either.

"I know you are, Jace. I love you. But I'm honestly fine."

I continue watching the TV. I know what day it is tomorrow, but I was hoping Jace might have forgotten about it. I don't want to talk about it, and I don't want him treating me as if I will break.

Bridge always rings me or pops around on the day too. I had lost my nan the previous year, and my dad has never been around. Being an only child sucks because now I have no family. I have an uncle, but he wasn't close with my mom, so I rarely speak to him. That's why I love Bridge, she feels like my aunt, even a second mom sometimes. Without Jace and his family and my friends, I have no idea where I'd be, but I can't imagine it would be a good place.

Chaper 11

I thought it was best I came into the office today instead of staying at home. As I walk through our office doors, I'm met straight away by my colleague, Rachel, holding a coffee outstretched in her hand with a huge smile on her face. She is a dream and the best colleague a girl could ask for. If you're behind on work, or just generally need help, she's your girl. She has stayed in the office with me past midnight before for clients that weren't even her own, but she knew if she didn't, I would be here until the following morning. That's the kind of girl she is. She is also one of my closest friends.

I flash a big grin to her.

"You're my lifesaver, thank you so much. You don't understand how much I need this," I say as I grab the takeaway cup out of her hand.

I work from home most days, but when I come into the office, she always has a takeaway coffee waiting for me.

"I missed you," she says as she pulls me in for a hug, avoiding the coffee in my hand.

"I missed you too, Rach," I say as we walk side by side to my office.

"What's your morning looking like?" I ask her with a smirk. She knows when I'm not in the office I miss out on a lot of the goss, and believe it or not, a lot goes on in this accounting firm. So when I am in the office, we always book an hour out in our schedules in the morning for a "work catch-up," when, in fact, it's her telling me everything that has happened and what I have missed.

She opens the door to my office and gives me a mischievous smile. I look over at my desk, and sitting there are two plates with my favorite pastries from my favorite bakery down the road.

"I already checked both of our schedules and saw we had a spare hour first thing this morning." She winks.

"You're the best, you know that."

The cinnamon hits my nose before I even arrive at my desk. *Ahh, my favorite coffee cake with cinnamon crumble.* This girl knows me too well.

We sit down and dig into our pastries and sip our coffee. I should come to the office more. Being at home is a lot more stressful and quite isolating. I love working here and love all my colleagues. Though, I wouldn't get this treatment if I came in all the time, so I think I will stick to popping in now and then.

I raise my eyebrows up to Rachel while she is stuffing her face with a waffle, and I laugh. "You enjoying that?"

She holds her mouth, trying to hold her laugh in without spitting her food out. She takes a big swallow before washing some down with her coffee.

"As soon as I laid it out on your desk, I wanted to dig in but had to wait for your ass, do you know the torture of it just sitting there and smelling the way it does."

"Okay, well now that you got your taste, spill, I want it all."

She nods, finishing another mouthful.

"I slept with Harley," she rushes out. I'm taken aback so much I choke.

Rachel leans over, smacking my back. I get myself under control and grab the napkin, dabbing at my mouth.

I look up at her with wide eyes. "You what!?" I shriek.

"Shhh, keep it down, will you?"

"Harley? Really?"

"I know, I know. It was one of the nights we were here late and—"

"Wait, wait, wait. You banged Harley in the office!?" I smile, this is by far the juiciest gossip I have had since working here.

"Ry, you cannot say a word." She points at me, trying to hold a stern face.

"As if I would. However, I need every scrap of detail, or I'll go ask Harley," I sass.

Rachel squints at me. "I should have done this over drinks. Why did I blurt that out over pastries and coffee, who does that?" She slumps her head on the desk.

I wrap my hands around the top of her bun and pull on it so she sits up.

"You're not getting away with this. Spill, right now!"

She sighs. "Okay, well . . ."

She takes a sip of her coffee, trying to prolong this as much as possible, so I lean across and take the coffee from her as well as her pastries. She glares at me as a kid would if their mom took their favorite toy away.

I fold my arms and raise an eyebrow at her. "You will get it back once you have told me everything."

She throws her arms up in the air. "Ahh, okay. Yes, we slept together in the office, on his desk, if you must know. Well, not on it, me over it with him behind me . . . But this isn't the first time."

I stare at her, my eyes wide. "What, well how many times? Rachel, how long has this been going on for?"

I peek down at her lap, through my glass desk, and she's twisting her ring around her fingers. This is not like Rachel; she is as loud and confident as they come. Her and Toni together are like a volcano erupting, two of the loudest personalities—it's enough to give you a migraine sometimes, believe me.

I lean over, placing my hand on the desk in front of her with my palm up, offering her to place her hand in mine. She does and squeezes before looking up with tears in her eyes. *Oh shit.*

I let go of her hand and walk around the desk, leaning down in front of her as a single tear runs down her face.

"Rach, shit. What's happened?" I don't know whether to ask, but I can't just leave it. "Has he . . . has he hurt you? You know you can tell me," I rush the last bit out.

She shakes her head back and forth fast. "No, no. Nothing like that." I grab a tissue and pass it to her.

"Talk to me, babe."

"There's so much to talk about, Ry. I honestly don't even know where to start." With how upset she is, I definitely think coffee and pastries are not the correct setting.

"How about we have this catch-up and you can tell me all about it over a liquid lunch? I think that will be better, don't you," I say, squeezing her hand.

She laughs while dabbing under her eyes, careful not to rub the makeup off.

"I think you're right, there. I'm sorry I just blurted it out like that, then cried on you. I just needed to get it off my chest, it's been playing on me for months now."

Months? Wow. I softly smile at her.

"I'm just glad you told me. You know I'm always here for you and will help you with anything."

"I know, Rylee, and thank you."

I walk around my desk, taking a seat, passing her back her coffee and pastries. We leave the gossip, as I don't think Rach is really in the mood, but we talk about how work has been. She tells me about some awkward clients who were causing her a lot of hassle, as they weren't giving her the information needed to accomplish the work—story of our lives. She asks me a few questions about things she isn't sure on. We always have things pop up that we need to bounce off each other to make sure we are taking the right approach.

"Okay, I think that's everything." She starts grabbing the trash, but I tell her to leave it. She smiles at me.

"I'll book a table for us at Chimes at say, 12:30? I'm thinking we could grab some food too?" I say as I load the website up, ready to book.

"That sounds perfect! Thanks again, Ry." She slips out of my office door.

I hope she is okay. I can't believe she hasn't told me about this before. I can only imagine this goes deeper than I may think and just pray Harley doesn't hurt her. He is known as the "office slut." He has the appearance for it, don't get me wrong. Swept back light-brown hair, bright-green eyes, chiseled jaw, and always looks immaculate and lives and breathes at the gym. There is one thing that makes all that come crashing down, well, for me, he knows he's hot and that is the biggest ick. Walks around the office like girls would sell their soul for five minutes to be with him, and it kills me a little inside every time I see him acting the way he does. He knows not to be like that around me, Jace made sure of that.

When I started working here, we had been together for about a year. Jace came and picked me up from work one day and saw Harley acting the way he does, so he made it very obvious I was taken, and that would not change, by kissing the life out of me right in front of my whole office. Jace has never been a jealous person, but I think he wanted to make a point that day. Harley, who used to flirt with me before this, backed away after that and treated me as a colleague, although we are all pretty relaxed around each other and treat each other more as friends, but he never swayed from that. I know how he can be, and I can bet any amount of money he has been playing with Rach's feelings.

I open my laptop, going through my emails. There are way too many, and I'm sure some of our clients think we work seven days a week because the amount I have from yesterday is a joke. *It's a Sunday. Give a girl a break.* I never knew all those years ago when I completed my degree in accountancy that there would be so much more to uncover within the job, and believe me, there is. We get hit with new challenges all the time but it's what makes the job interesting.

People would say accounting and interesting wouldn't go in the same sentence, but when you have a great team, it can make work interesting and enjoyable. It can also be a very stressful role, so having a great team alongside you makes all the difference, and here at Quaylands Accountancy, we have just that.

Quaylands is a global firm and has offices all around the world, so we have to be on our game at all times. We do have goals we have to reach, which makes it that more challenging, but like I say, we work as a team to hit those goals, and we do it with flying colors each time. We deal with a lot of corporate clients, so we deal with the larger company accounts, and most of our clients are great.

I go through my emails and reply to some. I need to get my spreadsheets open and work on some final accounts for one of our biggest clients. It's their financial year-end which always causes stress around the office. You can tell when this time of the year hits for this client as everyone is a lot more quiet and has their head down, focusing on the work. We have virtual meetings each week to go over what we're doing and who needs help with what. We set each person on one job so we're not crossing over on anything. It makes everything run smoothly.

A knock comes on my office door.

"Come in!"

The door opens and all I see are a huge bunch of multicolored tulips. My eyes grow big as I see the true size of them once poor Amelia, our receptionist, who is peeking over the top, walks up to my desk. I get up and walk around the front, taking them from her and placing them on my desk. Amelia flashes her beautiful big smile at me.

"These arrived via courier for you just now. They are beautiful." She beams.

"They really are, they're my favorites, so I can only guess who they're from." I smile back at her.

"I keep telling you, you need to hook me up with one of Jace's friends, Rylee. I need this kind of treatment in my life." She giggles as she heads toward the door.

I laugh back at her. "If he had any decent single friends, you would be the first person I would be contacting, but unfortunately, he doesn't at the moment. They are all taken." That's not necessarily true, but Jace's friends are still going through their whore stage. I don't need to be having them break my colleague's heart. There is James, who I did consider for a moment, but to be honest, I think Amelia can do better.

Amelia opens my door and turns around to me.

"Typical, always the way," she huffs as she walks out.

I stare at the flowers and see a note tucked in the top of the bouquet. I pick it out and *Ry Bear* is handwritten on the front.

I open the envelope and look at the front of the card. It's two bears cuddling with a big heart-shaped balloon behind them. I smile as I open the card.

To my Ry Bear,

Life didn't make sense before you. You gave it a reason.

I didn't know what love meant before you. You gave it a meaning.

My life was in darkness before you came. You gave it light.

When I was weak, you gave me strength.

When I thought I couldn't be loved. You gave me you.

You don't realize how much of a shining star you are in people's lives, Ry.

It's us. Jace and Rylee. Always. Forever.

I'm sobbing by the time I finish reading the note. *How can he be so perfect?* I know why he did this today, he wanted to remind me I always have him, no matter what. He wanted to make me smile on a day I should be sad. I read the note again and cry more. I cry out of happiness that I found someone like Jace in such a random way, and how he just came into my life without a care in the world and told me he would be seeing me again. I cry for my mom, it's things like this she would scream and squeal down the phone at.

Jace is everything she could ever want for me. She wanted to see me get married to someone that truly worshipped the ground I walk on, and she wanted me to give her grandbabies she could dote on. I always said I wasn't sure on having a baby, but she knew Jace would be the father of my children. She loved him so much, and she got to see me happy, but her dream was to see me walking down the aisle. Although none of that has happened yet, Jace and I have talked about it a lot and it is something that will be in our future. I hope she's looking down at this now and can see how happy he makes me and how special he is.

I grab my phone off my desk and open up Jace's conversation on WhatsApp.

> Me: You have me crying happy tears. When did I get so lucky? Thank you so much. I love you, Jace. Always. Forever.

I would normally ring him, but I know he has an important meeting today, so I don't want to interrupt him.

As I have a lot to finish for this year-end, I will be in the office a lot, so I will keep the flowers here, but I take a picture of them and send them to Toni. She always jokes around that me and Jace make her sick with our love for each other, but we all know she is only joking. She was so happy for me when I started seeing Jace. They get along like brother and sister, and I know they love each other.

I place the flowers on my side table. They're beautiful in my office, and he knows how much I love tulips, especially when they have been dip-dyed in multiple colors. They are so pretty. I return to my laptop. I best get started on this work before heading to lunch with Rach.

Chapter 12

A few hours later, Rach walks straight into my office. She's standing there with her bag and coat on, ready for our lunch.

"You ready?"

"Give me two secs, let me just finish this email." Rach walks over to the flowers. I read over my email quickly before sending and then close my laptop down and grab my coat and bag.

Rach has a huge smile on her face. "Are these from Jace?"

"Nope, they're from his dad."

Her face drops. "What? Why would Cash be sending you flowers?"

I burst out laughing. "Of course they're from Jace. Who else would they be from?" I roll my eyes.

"I was about to say, you best not be playing away with my Jace's daddy now, Ry." I look at her with an are-you-serious face. She laughs it off while we head toward the door. As well as Toni and Jace having an amazing bond, Rach and Jace also do. They are as good as best friends, and annoyingly, she always takes his side if I'm in a mood. She says, "*Stop being mean to my Jace*," and, of course, Jace laps it up. I love the bond he has with two of my closest friends, though, it makes life easier. There would be nothing worse than the friends you love the most not getting on with one of the other people you love the most. I'm lucky because everyone gets on well. Rach and Ton hit it off when I brought Rach out with me on our nights out after working here for a while. Three's a crowd was never a problem for us!

Chimes is only around the corner, so instead of grabbing a taxi, we take a walk.

"You don't understand how much I need this drink." Steam flows out of her mouth to show how cold it is.

"That bad, huh?" I ask.

"You have no idea," she huffs.

Within five minutes of walking, we are outside Chimes. After telling them our reservation, we are shown to our seats. It's not a posh place, by any means, but it's nice and quiet. I thought we would need somewhere like this for the chat. I also asked when I booked if we could have a particular table that is hidden away at the back of the restaurant. I want Rach to have her privacy, and if she needs to cry, I don't want her holding it in.

We sit down and immediately pick up the food menu. Food is life, we always say, we look at food and then the drinks. However, I have already checked the menu out online and picked what I am having, because who doesn't do that? I always scan the menu, though, just to make sure I don't fancy something else or I missed something.

Rach being my soul sister puts the menu down. "I don't know why I'm looking like I didn't pick what I was having three hours ago."

I throw my head back on a laugh. "Same girl, same! What are you having?"

"I'm going with the Chimes loaded burger and fries. I need all the grease to make me happy."

"I'm sure we were separated at birth because I'm having that too. Did you see the picture online, it looks insane."

"The picture is what sold it for me, I didn't even check to see what was in it." She laughs.

We laugh while the waiter comes over and asks us what we want to order. Rach tells him we know what drinks and food we want. We always get a bottle of sauvignon when we're out. It's our go-to wine.

"So . . ." I say.

"At least let the wine arrive, Ry." She rolls her eyes, then smirks.

"Okay, okay." I make small talk while we wait for the wine to arrive, talking about how work has gone this morning. Rach had a virtual meeting with the directors of the corporate company we are doing the year-end for to see if they have all the information we need to do the audits. Of course they didn't but we expect this every year, you can tell yourself until you're blue in the face that everything will run on time, everything will be done to deadline, but I can promise you, that never happens.

Our wine arrives and the waiter pours us half a glass, and as he walks off, Rach grabs the bottle out of the ice bucket and tops hers off.

"Erm, am I shit on your shoe?" I raise my eyebrow at her.

"Sorry, I wasn't sure if you had a lot of work to get back to." Once she fills my glass to the top, she places the bottle back down and gulps her drink.

I wait patiently, not wanting to push her or stress her out because it's obvious the whole ordeal has her emotional.

"So, a few months back, I don't remember what date and time exactly, before you ask." I smirk, she knows me so well. I'm extra as fuck sometimes, I can't help it.

"I was working late on that company's, Braders, accounts. You know the really awkward ones that just weren't helping us in any way."

I nod along because, yes, I remember those, they had me up to all hours of the morning, and it didn't help they were in London either, so the time difference made it worse. Our London office wasn't able to deal with it as Braders also has American accounts, but their head office is in London.

"Well, I was cursing them, you know when they wind you up so much, you are literally screaming at the computer." I laugh because this is me at least twice a month.

"Then I heard someone clearing their throat behind me, and Harley was standing at my office door, smirking. He found it funny the amount of shit I was saying and actually thought I was on the phone to a boyfriend or ex. Anyway, I explained to him about the clients and then he was telling me about some awkward ones he had in the past, then offered to help. We have a great team and always offer to help each other, so I was really grateful.

"He worked with me until half past two in the morning. I couldn't thank him enough, halfway through he even went and got a secret stash he had in his drawer of bourbon. We were sipping that, and the next thing I know, I was lying back on my desk while he was stripping me out of my clothes. Honestly, it's all a bit broken up. I thought we would just come into the office the next day and forget it happened, but he wasn't letting it go that easily, and we continued to hook up.

"Now I very stupidly have feelings for him. He says all the right things but then will go two days ignoring me. Oh, and lets also add the way he still flirts with every fucking girl in the office but will have me bent over my desk on his lunch break," she rushes out, now red in the face through anger and possibly a little embarrassment.

I stare at her for a minute, taking in everything she said.

"Uh-huh. Okay," I say as I don't really know what to say.

Her mouth drops. "'Uh-huh, okay' is all you have to say right now, Ry? Really?"

"Shit on a stick, give me a minute to process all this information," I say while she downs the rest of her glass and then fills it up again. She then waves the waiter down for another bottle. *Oh boy.*

"Okay, well the fact it's carried on, it's not Harley, from what we know. You know he always goes on about that cringy one-night rule. The fact he is playing with you, though, Rach, doesn't sit right with me. You work together as well, you don't want this affecting your job. I don't think I have ever seen this many different emotions with you in one day either." I purse my lips. If I could ring this boy's neck, I would, however, Rach is going along with it, what guy would say no? They need their heads banged together, but she is a little fragile, so I won't word it that way.

"Honestly, Ry—" She sighs. "I don't ever remember having this many emotions. I'm doing that cringe shit girls do when they check the guy's Instagram and Facebook to see if they are out and who they're with, what girls they're with. That's not me, and you know it's not."

"Girl . . . you need to have a chat with him and tell him what's what. You either put your feelings clear on a plate for him or you just end things. If he backs away when you admit your feelings, then you know what we already thought. He is a great colleague but a total fuck boy when it comes to women."

She laughs but at the same time her eyes well with tears. I just want to hug her, but I know when you're in this moment, hugging makes it so much worse.

"I just know for a fact, what you just said about us knowing what we knew all along, that's going to be the end result, and it scares me, Ry. It will break me if he laughs in my face or tells me he doesn't feel the same. I have real feelings for him, Ry. Trust me to get feelings for a fuck boy." She rolls her eyes, trying to hold her tears at bay.

"If he dared laugh in your face, I would make his workdays a living hell. Just so you know. Also, I reckon 'your' Jace will have a thing or two to say to him," I tease, trying to make her smile.

She grabs my hand on the table and squeezes. "I know you would, Ry, and I know Jace would, but I wouldn't want a big deal made out of it. I would be embarrassed enough." She sighs.

"How about we forget about Fuck Boy H for now, because that is his new nickname until he sorts his shit out, and you tell me about all the other goss I know you probably have building inside that brain of yours." I wink at her.

She makes a big sigh and smiles big at me. "You know me well, because I have been dying to tell you what happened with Libby and Mark last week," she says all big-eyed like a kid at Christmas. I can already tell her mind is drifting away from Harley, and this is exactly what is needed.

We continue chatting and gossiping, and next thing we know, we have devoured our loaded burgers and drank through two bottles of wine. To say I'm feeling tipsy is an understatement. Thank God the big boss is not in today because I can imagine he wouldn't be impressed if Rach and I walk back into the office tipsy.

"C'mon, we need to get back." *How the hell am I supposed to work on numbers while feeling like this*? I may just catch up on emails I need to reply to, I don't trust myself with numbers at the moment.

Rach giggles while putting on her coat. "Thank God, Fuck Boy H isn't in the office today because the way I'm feeling right now, I would literally go into his office and tell him to go fuck himself."

"More like let him bend you over his desk," I mutter.

She gasps, and has her hand against her chest like I wounded her. She then breaks into giggles.

"We both know me over his desk is a much more likely option." She laughs.

We walk out of the restaurant arm-in-arm, giggling our way back to the office. Rachel doesn't even realize how much she has helped me today.

Chapter 13

I walk into my apartment, chucking my bag on the floor and removing my heels, then let out the biggest sigh. It's like taking your bra off after a long day. I had to sober myself when we got back in the office. Somehow, my inbox doubled in size while I was at lunch. I told Jace I would be home about six but it's seven thirty. The time got away with me replying to emails. It wasn't until Jace called me at half past six that I realized the time.

"Jace!" I shout through the apartment.

"In here, babe," he shouts from the kitchen.

I walk in the kitchen and the smell of whatever he is cooking assaults my senses. I walk over and peep around his shoulder.

"No peeking," he says while pushing me away. "Go get yourself out of your work clothes. Dinner will be ready in about forty minutes."

I smile at him. "Okay. I will take a quick shower and get changed."

Once I'm out, I clip my wet hair back in a messy half-up, half-down style and let it dry naturally. I have a natural wave to my hair, so normally it dries nice as long as I put anti-frizz serum on it. I chuck on a skater-style dress and apply a bit of mascara.

"Ry, dinner is ready," Jace shouts from the dining room.

I apply some lip gloss and walk down the hallway to the dining room. I could smell the food while I was getting ready, and it has my mouth watering. I walk into the dining room and am stunned at how beautiful it is. Jace has three bunches of tulips, like the ones he sent me earlier—one sitting in the middle of the table, the other two on each of the side tables in the corners—and the light is dimmed, and there are candles everywhere. Our food is set out on the plate, and it is our favorite dish: chicken-bacon pasta baked in a white wine creamy sauce. With my favorite white wine.

"You're so perfect, you know that."

"Come sit, baby."

He pulls the chair out for me, and I sit as he leans over, filling my wineglass. Jace takes a seat opposite me.

"Not that I'm complaining, Jace, but what is all this for?"

"I just wanted you to know how important you are to me, Ry. I hope that I do show you every day, but I like to just make sure sometimes. I didn't want you being sad today, I wanted you to be happy. You don't understand how beautiful you are when you're happy. Everyone needs to see you smile." He is so confident with his words, and I have never known someone who is so expressive with their feelings. I'm getting emotional. I know what today is but he's trying to take my mind off it by doing all this, and it does. It has.

"Thank you," I say, trying to keep my tears at bay.

"Let's eat before it gets cold," he says.

We eat and chat about our day. I fill Jace in on what happened between Rach and Harley. I can tell he's not happy with Harley. They have a close bond, so he's somewhat protective over Rach. She would be so happy seeing the way Jace is now. She is an only child and always said she felt like he was a big brother to her.

Jace tells me that work is calming down and he is starting not to dread going in. He mentions he has a meeting late tomorrow night in the city but shouldn't be home too late. We finished eating our dinner and it was amazing. One thing Jace never let on for a while was how much of a good cook he was. We both are, to be honest, and sometimes we love opening a recipe book and cooking a big meal together.

I walk around the table, and Jace has turned his chair so I'm facing him. I grab his face with both hands and lean down, dropping a soft kiss to his lips.

"Thank you so much for this, for today. The flowers, the note, the dinner." Jace leans up, chasing my lips. My lips meet his once again, this time parting. I angle my head to the side while Jace slips his tongue in my mouth. The kiss has gone from slow to urgent. I straddle Jace's lap, and he stands, and before I know it, he's laying me on the table, avoiding the plates and cutlery.

I lie back and wrap my legs around his waist, and he kisses down my neck. His hands move to pull my dress up my body. I sit up slightly, making it easier for him to lift it over my head, then he throws it behind me. He grabs my face and kisses me again, but I break the kiss and pull his top up and over his head.

We move in sync, our mouths clashing together in a frenzy. We could go to the bedroom, but I need him now. I can't wait.

Jace pushes on my shoulder, laying me flat on the table. He undoes his jeans and doesn't even tug them all the way down, then pulls his dick out. He strokes his hard dick up and down. I don't take my eyes off him, mesmerized by the angry veins running over it.

I go to sit up, and he commands, "No. Lay down.

"I love you so fucking much, Ry. Never forget that," Jace whispers to my lips as he slides into me. He leans on his forearms, kissing me like he is starved for me. He lazily slides in and out, taking his time like he is savoring every inch of me. We break apart, staring into each other's eyes as he makes love to me. At this moment, there is no place on earth I would rather be.

Soft, warm lips press against my head, sending a tingle and heat through me. I squint my eyes open. Jace is dressed in his suit, smiling at me.

"What time is it?" I yawn out.

"Eight, babe. You're working from home today, right?"

"Yeah. What time will you be home tonight roughly. Will you be having dinner?"

"Don't worry about that. It will probably be late in the evening. I will text you when I know what time, okay?" he says, stroking the top of my head.

I nod at him as I yawn again, burying my head further into the pillow.

"Thank you for yesterday, Jace." I smile up at him, struggling to keep my eyes open. I'm exhausted.

He leans down, kissing me on the lips. "Anything for you. Have a good day. I love you, baby."

"Always?" I say, closing my eyes.

The warmth of Jace's breath caresses my ear. "Forever."

My day has dragged. I rolled out of bed this morning and just about crawled into our office to grab my laptop and bring it back to bed. I had no energy. I ended up getting out of bed about 11:00 a.m., but I'm still sitting in my pj's and robe. I just can't be bothered today. My phone rings and it's Toni.

"Hey," I mumble.

"Yo, bitchface," she yells down the phone, because Toni speaking a normal level is a rarity in this lifetime.

"What's up?" I say in a loud yawn.

"No. You're making me tired, I'm starting to catch the yawn, and we don't want to catch the yawn, we want to catch vibbees," she rushes out.

"Come again?" I say because everything she said went way over my head. Her hyper moods are wild sometimes.

"Wake up," she says way too loudly. "I called to find out if you found out what is going on with James and Jace and why Daddy acted the way he did?"

I roll my eyes at the Daddy comment. She always calls Cash, Daddy because she said he is the ultimate "Daddy." Every time she's around him, she flirts up a storm, which embarrasses the hell out of me. She even asked him one time, when she was drunk, if he was single and looking for a pet. *I was mortified!* She shrugged and laughed it off the following day, and I can't say Cash ever looked at her the same again.

I sit there for a minute, confused as to how she knew but then remembered I texted her yesterday after she texted me with heart emojis to show me she knew what day it was. She didn't say anything, and I appreciated that. I then dropped her a quick text telling her briefly what happened and that I would call her today, but I forgot.

"Oh no, I forgot."

"Ahh, okay." She moans. "Well, have a good day, ring me tonight when you know."

"I swear you just use me for gossip," I tease.

"Bitch, please." She laughs. "You have gossip like once a year."

"You bit—"

"Baaa, love you," she says before hanging up and not letting me finish.

I laugh, shaking my head and placing the phone back down on my desk. That girl has some nerve, she is lucky I love her so much.

By 6:00 p.m., I'm done with work. I haven't heard from Jace all day, but I know he had a few important meetings, so I'm guessing he's tied up. I still feel like I haven't slept a wink, and luckily there is leftover dinner from last night. I know Jace will not be back until late, so I may as well have an early night instead of trying to stay awake.

An hour later, I'm in bed, struggling to keep my eyes open. I had dinner, then a quick shower. I don't remember the last time I went to bed this early, but hopefully I feel better tomorrow. I turn to my side, leaning up slightly to turn the bedside lamp off. I lay my head on the pillow, closing my eyes, knowing I will be out like a light within seconds.

CHAPTER 14

I'm woken to my mobile ringing on the bedside table, and I see it's 1:46 a.m. Jace isn't in bed. *What the hell?*

I pick my phone up and see the caller ID. *Why is Cash calling me?* I answer the phone quickly.

"Cash?" I say uncertainly.

"Rylee. I-I need you to get down to Baltimore General, now. It's Jace, he's . . ."

I put the phone down, flying out of bed. I don't need to hear anymore. Jace is in the hospital. *What the fuck happened?* I chuck on a jumper, leaving my pj pants on. I don't care what I look like right now. I need to get to Jace. I step into my trainers, grab my keys, and run straight out the door.

I'm walking through the hospital doors, not even knowing how I got here. I don't actually remember the drive. Jace is the only thing on my mind. I need to see him and make sure he's okay. I can't think about anything else until I've seen him.

I walk up to the reception desk. "Jace Stiles," I say to the lady. "My boyfriend. Jace Stiles, he was brought here tonight. I-I don't know what happened but he's here, where is he?" I say, my hands shaking. I just want to see him.

"Bear with me a minute, miss," the lady says while looking at her computer. I'm pacing up and down, waiting for what feels like years for this woman to tell me where Jace is.

"Miss!" I snap my head over to the woman. She's observing me with a small but sympathetic smile that has my heart skyrocketing out of my chest and legs feeling like deadweights.

"He's in the ICU," she gently says.

I stare at her, not moving.

"D-did you?" I'm trying to take breaths but it's hard to breathe. "Intensive care?" Tears run down my face.

This can't be true. No, my Jace is not in the ICU, no way. He can't be, they must have the wrong person. I glance up at the receptionist. "Sorry, I said Jace Stiles, I don't think you got that right."

Her shoulders drop as her features soften. She offers a small smile, then her eyes glance over my right shoulder. "Excuse me, miss" comes from behind me, and I spin around to a man standing there.

"Let me show you where you need to go." I nod, following him on autopilot. I'm walking but I don't know how. Everything feels like it's moving in slow motion around me, but I'm anxious, my heart is beating in my throat, the sickness is sitting there waiting to come up. *Am I in a dream right now?*

"Miss." A soothing tone breaks through my thoughts. I glance up at the man who has a hand out to the side, gesturing to two double white doors.

"The waiting room is through that door, you—"

I'm already walking away from the man, I need to see what's going on. I burst through the double door and see their ashen faces, which highlights their red swollen eyes as they all glance up at me.

"Nooo," I whisper, shaking my head.

Bridget comes running toward me. "I need to know what's happened, please. Wh-where is he?" I ask, barely holding myself together.

Bridget wraps her arms around me, sniffling. Her body jolts as she cries into my shoulder.

"He was in a-a car accident, Ry. Jace," she cries out. "He is in a coma," she shrieks not being able to control her sobs.

The floor crumbles beneath me. Everything around me goes lopsided as my vision goes fuzzy. I claw at my neck, trying to rid of the invisible rope binding its way around my throat, cutting off my oxygen. Two hands grip my arms and sit me down.

"Breathe, Rylee." Bohdi's voice grounds me, bringing my vision back. I stare into his bloodshot eyes that make the blue stand out more, his tears welling, ready to drop with one blink. Boh kneels in front of me, not saying anymore, but the pain in his eyes is too much to bear, so I look to the floor, focusing on a smudge mark.

"Can you just—" I take a deep breath. "Just tell me where he is," I say while the tears pour down my face.

I look back up at Boh and then glance over his shoulder to Bridget. Bridget's eyes avert to a room with a shut door. I'm standing up, my legs are carrying me toward the door before I can even think. Bridget says something to Boh, probably trying to stop me, but I move with speed. I need to see him. I see Cash from the corner of my eye trying to grab me, which I veer away from and burst through the door.

"Oh God." I raise my hand to my mouth, trying to keep the sickness at bay that threatened to rise. I stand there stunned, staring at a person I don't recognize lying in the hospital bed. That's not Jace.

My view is blocked by someone.

"Miss, Miss." Their lips are moving but I can't hear what they're saying. I look up from the person's lips to their eyes. Sympathy. That's all I see. Someone's fingers bite into my skin around my arms and causes me to snap out of my trance.

"You can't just barge in here, Rylee," Cash spits with pure anger as he drags me out of the room. I take one last look at the person in the bed. It's not Jace.

"What the fuck do you think you're doing, Rylee, they can't do their job if you just barge in there. We are all waiting for news, not just you!" he shouts.

I look Cash in his eyes, moving from one to the other, and he appears like he has aged ten years since I saw him last.

"What are you talking about. That's not Jace," I say, pointing toward the room. I move my gaze from him to Bridget. Cash's anger drops from his face and gets replaced with exhaustion. Bridget walks over to me, bringing her hands on either side of my arms, walking me away from Cash. *What is wrong with them? It's not Jace.* I look at Bridget, hoping she will back me up like she always does.

"Rylee, let's go get coffee." Bridget pulls me toward the doors.

We walk toward the coffee machine in silence. When we get to the coffee machine, I go to ask why they think it's Jace.

"He will pull through this, Ry. Our Jace is built of the strong stuff," she says, as if she's trying to convince herself.

"It's not Jace," I whisper.

It can't be Jace. That wasn't my Jace in there. My heart speeds up. *Why don't I just go home?* I'm sure this is a big misunderstanding. Jace will be at home. *Right?*

I follow Bridge back into the waiting room. I don't know why my body won't let me leave the hospital even though my brain is screaming for me to go home. There is a feeling in my stomach that's keeping me here, and I don't know why.

As we enter the waiting room, Cash is in what seems like a deep discussion with the doctor that stood in front of me in the room. Bridget rushes over. There's tears in Bridget's and Cash's eyes. I walk over and hear the tail end of the conversation.

"You may go and see him now." Cash nods and thanks the doctor.

Cash holds Bridget's hand, she's trembling as she reaches for my hand.

"Are you ready, Ry?"

I nod absently, my body just agreeing and letting Bridget drag me toward the door. I know it's not Jace in there, but it's like my body doesn't believe it.

Cash enters first and freezes. Tears pour down his face as he continues to walk into the room. Boh takes a deep breath and places his hand on Cash's shoulder, offering his support in silence. Bridget lets out a delayed sob, bringing her hand to her mouth, as if she was not believing what she was seeing at first. Cash turns around, bringing Bridget into his arms and holding her while she uncontrollably sobs into his chest. Cash is now looking straight at me as his bottom lip wobbles. I'm struggling to step over the threshold, one more step and I will see that face again. The one that isn't Jace.

I take a deep breath, taking the step but keeping my eyes locked with Cash's. I break away from the stare and look to my right. The sight is awful. There are bandages wrapped around the person's head. The little bit of skin showing on their face is cut up and bruised. I stare longer, it's not Jace, there is no nose ring. I then look back at Cash and Bridget who slowly make their way toward the bed. There are tubes and wires everywhere. I stay frozen to my spot, not being able to move anymore. I zone out, staring at the life-support machine, and all I can hear are sniffles and beeping.

I cast my eyes to Cash with his head in his hands. His shoulders are shaking, and Bridget is staring at the person with tears pouring out of her eyes. It's then the numbness starts to subside, I feel sick, and my heart is beating erratically. A hot flush comes over my whole body.

I close my eyes and take deep breaths.

"It's not Jace. It's not Jace. It's not Jace," I chant to myself quietly.

"Shut up!"

I snap my eyes open. Cash is standing in front of me with utter rage in his eyes.

"The sooner you come to terms with this, Rylee, the easier for all of us." Cash steps to the side and points at the person in the bed.

"That's my son!" he screams in my face.

"Cash, stop!" Bridget cries behind him.

Cash pushes his hands through his hair, pulling at his roots as he walks back to the chair. Bridget rubs his back while staring at me, her chin trembles as more tears run down over her red, blotchy skin.

My body shakes as I drift my eyes away from them and onto the bed. It's then I notice the person's hand, my stare moves up their arm and then I stop, looking across to the other arm. Jace has the letter *R* tattooed on his wrist and I have the letter *J*. I can't see under their wrist, so I walk over with trembling hands, turn their wrist over, and see the *R*. I line my wrist up with theirs, and see the *J*. I stare at both wrists. J & R. Jace and Rylee.

"No, no, nooo!" I scream out. I look up at his face, trying to see through the overflowing tears. *Where is my beautiful boy?* His face is so broken, I don't even recognize him.

I double over, dropping to the floor beside him . . . the pain, it hurts so much. My heart physically aches. Two arms wrap around me and pull me to stand. I don't open my eyes. It feels too real when they're open.

I lay my head on a solid chest, crying uncontrollably.

"It's okay, Rylee." Cash's deep voice breaks through my crying.

I break out of his hold and stare up at him, seeing my hurt mirrored in his eyes.

Anger invades me.

"Why did you let me see him like this? This is not my Jace!"

Bridget breaks out in more sobs, and instead of anger on Cash's face, I see hurt. He's hurting because his son, who doesn't look like his son, is lying in a coma in front of him while a machine breathes for him.

"Why, Cash? Why!?" I scream and cry.

He grabs hold of me and pulls me to his chest, holding me tight. *No. I don't want him holding me. I want Jace.*

"Get off me!" I try and wiggle out of his hold and punch at his chest.

"Let me go. I don't want you. I want Jace." I sob. Cash doesn't let go. He just holds me tighter while I keep trying to punch my way out of his hold.

My strength is lost when it really sinks in.

Jace is on life support in a coma, and I don't know if he will ever wake up from it.

In that moment, my body goes weak. I can't feel my legs. Cash is the only thing holding me up while he squeezes me tight, caressing the back of my head.

I sob, I sob so hard I can barely breathe. I turn my head to the right while still resting on Cash's chest, looking at my beautiful boy. I just want him to open those eyes so I can see his gorgeous blue eyes that light up every room. It's in that moment that my heart shatters into tiny pieces, and the only person who can put it back together is Jace.

For the first time, I sob out, "It's my Jace."

Chater 15

I sit beside Jace's hospital bed, holding his hand, taking comfort in the warmth soaking into my skin. I can't see much of his face due to all the bandages, but what I can see, I'm holding onto. I keep hoping his eyes flicker or give some sign that he's here, with us. Cash is fast asleep on the other side of the bed.

I don't even know what time it is, but I can't fall asleep. What if he wakes and needs urgent medical assistance? I need to be here for him. Bridget went home as they said only two people could stay with him. I made it clear I was not going anywhere. There is no way I can leave Jace's side. I keep praying I will wake up from this horrible dream, that I'll turn around and see his beautiful face and his blue eyes staring back at me.

The constant beeping is a reminder that I'm not dreaming and this is very much real. Cash and the doctors were talking earlier, I couldn't hear the exact words being said but I know whatever the doctors were saying, Cash was either not happy with it or he didn't believe it. He stormed out of the room and when he returned, his face said he didn't have time to deal with me, so I have let it be, but I will speak to Bridget when she is back. I'm sure he told her. I didn't have the energy to argue with him.

I haven't heard much of what happened, but I heard car crash and fire. I don't think I want to know. It all hurts too much knowing my baby was in pain, knowing it was so traumatic for his body that his brain couldn't handle it.

Cash stirs and slowly opens his eyes, and the first place he looks is at Jace, probably hoping to see his eyes open. He then looks at me.

"What did the doctor say to you earlier?" As much as I don't want to know, I need to know what is going, I have every right to know. I need to know how serious this is.

Cash stares at me. He sits up more, leaning his arms on his knees as he drops his head to his hands. He stays like that for a few moments before lifting his head and running his hands over his face.

"They said the tests they ran showed a high dosage of Xanax and Valium in his system." He sighs.

I sit there for a moment, taking in what Cash said. Xanax and Valium? Jace has never taken those. *Nope. No way.* I have never known him to need it.

"That can't be right."

Cash nods. "I know, I said this to the doctor."

"There's more," he murmurs, staring down at the floor.

My breath hitches. "Go on," I say as the tears form in my eyes.

"The doctor said Jace sustained horrendous injuries. One being a bad trauma to the head. He . . . he." Tears fall from Cash's eyes.

"Cash? Please tell me," I say on the edge of hysteria.

"When they arrived at the scene . . ." He glances up at me and then over to Jace, more tears falling from his eyes.

"He was not breathing, Ry. My boy was not breathing." He breaks out in sobs, placing his head in his hands.

I can't move, I can't even look away from Cash after what he said. Jace stopped breathing. He died. I break out in a loud sob, running to the toilet and emptying my stomach. I turn to my side, dropping myself down next to the toilet. *Beep. Beep. Beep.* I close my eyes, the noise calming my insides. As long as I can always hear beeping, I know my baby is still there. He's still with us, fighting.

A few minutes later, someone enters the room. I rush out to see if it's the doctors, and Bohdi is standing there in complete shock, staring at Jace like it's the first time seeing him. I don't think it sunk in, seeing him earlier. It doesn't look like Jace, so I can see why it's hard to get your head around it. His eyes well with tears as he walks toward Cash, and Cash stands as Bohdi wraps him in a big hug. Cash softly cries into his shoulder, gripping Bohdi like he's his lifeline.

Someone enters the room, so I spin around, and I'm shocked to see two cops. *Why are they here?* Bohdi is quick to walk over to them.

"Can I help you?" Bohdi says.

The policeman pushes his hand out to Boh.

"I'm Officer Kenley, this is Officer Marcum," he replies. "Are you Cash Stiles?"

"No—"

"I am, can I help you?"

"Mr. Stiles, my colleague and I want to talk to you about the accident. Is there a room we can talk in?"

Boh butts in. "I don't think this is the time, can you come back another day?" Cash places his hand on Boh's shoulder.

"It's fine, brother." Normally Cash would have bit back, but I can tell he has no fight left in him, he probably wants to get it over with. Cash walks out the door with them.

They didn't ask to speak with me, but I need to know what happened. *Where was Jace coming from?* I know nothing about what happened. I haven't had the time to speak with anyone yet.

"Boh," I murmur. "What happened?"

Boh takes a long sigh, staring at Jace.

"I don't know much, Ry. He had a late meeting with some clients. He stopped off at a bar after with some friends, I haven't been told who." He looks down.

"He was on his way home. They think he fell asleep at the wheel."

I nod absently. The tears don't stop coming and are falling like a waterfall. I have so many questions, but the only person that can answer them is in a coma.

"Come here."

I run into Boh's arms, and he hugs me close to him while I sob into his chest.

"Why is this happening, Boh. I just want to wake up and this all be a dream."

"I know, Ry. I know. He will come back to us."

The door opens and this time it's Cash that walks in. I wait for the cops to walk in after him and ask to speak to me but they don't come. Boh and I are standing, waiting with bated breath for Cash to speak. It's like there is this tension and none of us want to speak first.

Cash breaks the silence. "They have gone," he states while walking over to a chair next to Boh and sitting, keeping his eyes solely on Jace. I'm relieved but confused as to why they didn't want to talk to me.

"What did they say?" Boh asks, biting his lip.

Cash lets out a big sigh, picking at lint that's not even there on his jeans. "They think it was some kind of freak accident. They are not ruling anything suspicious, and with the high dosage of Xanax and Valium in his system, they think he . . ." Cash gets up and paces the room, appearing like he has the weight of the world on his shoulders, and he probably does, I think that's how we all feel. "They didn't have to say what they thought," he grits out. "I can tell by their cryptic words that they want to consider it was done on purpose."

I shoot up out of my chair. "What? No," I let out. Tears form again in my eyes. "How can they even suggest that, Cash?" I look over to Jace, the tears bleeding from my eyes. That's how is feels with all the crying I have done. There is no way he would kill himself. He was so happy, he had everything. *Didn't he?* I break out into a loud sob, the pain slicing through my heart at even the thought of Jace not being happy and not telling me.

It doesn't make any sense why he had taken Xanax and Valium together or even at all. He has never mentioned being on them before. A warmth envelopes me, and I know it's Boh. I lean my head into his shoulder while he wraps his arm around me, cocooning me into him while I cry again. *When will this nightmare be over?* I keep running my eyes over Jace in the hope it somehow telepathically wakes him up. *Please wake up, Jace.*

The door opens again sometime later while we all sit around Jace's bed in silence. I recognize the doctor from yesterday. Bridget is back now. Bridge and I have been consoling each other over what Cash has relayed from the police. She agreed that it's not like Jace, and one of us would have known if he was taking those drugs. I feel a twinge in my heart when I think about it. *Was I too wrapped up in myself?* I don't think I ever have been but now I keep thinking back. *When did I ever ask Jace if he was okay, like really ask him. Was I too much to handle as a girlfriend that he had to take these?* I try and stop the thoughts and bring myself back to the present, but they keep playing in my head.

My heart jumps from my chest when Cash leaps up from his chair.

"Any news?" Cash asks the doctor. I'm praying he has some good news for us.

"Mr. Stiles, Ms. Matthews," the doctor says, then smiles at Bridget and Boh beside us. Cash and I are standing there staring at the doctor, waiting with bated breath. Bohdi places one hand on my shoulder as support. The doctor glances at Boh.

"That is Jace's uncle, Bohdi Stiles, he can hear whatever you are going to say."

The doctor nods. "Okay, but shall we sit down?"

"No, just tell us here. Now. Please," I add in, desperate for information about Jace.

He gives me a small smile.

"Okay, as you know, Jace suffered extreme trauma to his head that has caused swelling to his brain. This is one of the reasons why Jace fell in a coma. He also stopped breathing, and at this time, we cannot determine how long for, this can cause a lot of issues with the brain and having a trauma already mixed in with that." He stops to cast his eyes over all four of us. "We have run an EEG and various other tests, which focuses on Jace's brain activity, we currently have specialists reviewing this now and will hopefully have results by tomorrow morning." He takes a deep breath and looks at us directly. "I think you need to take each day as they come."

"So, what . . . what . . ." I can't get my words out. *What does he mean each day as it comes?* My head is spinning.

Cash is staring at the floor. "Cash," I whisper.

I look back up at the doctor. Everything feels like it's moving in slow motion.

"Are you saying that Jace may not wake up from the coma?" Bohdi breaks the silence. I'm praying the doctor doesn't confirm this is what he is saying.

The doctor ever so slightly nods. "I'm afraid so."

I stagger back, losing my footing. Someone catches me as I drop to the floor, lowering me gently. This cannot be happening, the imaginary rope binds its way around my neck again, and I struggle to catch my breath, all I see is dark shadows and hear quiet voices that sound far away. I close my eyes as my body slowly shuts down on me. I try to take a deep breath but it's no use, the blackness engulfs me, and I pray to the gods I have never prayed to a day in my life that when I open my eyes again, this is all a dream.

CHAPER 16

Beep. Beep. Beep. This noise relieved me before, but now it's a reminder of where I am and who is on the other end of that machine. I guess the gods didn't answer my prayers. It wasn't a dream.

I squint as a light temporarily blinds me. Bridget and Boh are kneeling beside me, their eyebrows drawn together, and eyes skating over my face as if they're looking for any injuries. Tears are freely falling from Bridget's eyes.

"Please tell me that was a dream?" I say to no one in particular.

Dr. Lane lowers his head to the floor.

"I think you will be okay. I know it's hard but try not to stress too much," he instructs. He helps me up off the floor, and I take a seat in the chair next to Jace.

I glance over at Jace, tears falling from my eyes. *How can I live without him?* There is no life without him in it. If Jace doesn't walk this planet, I don't know how I'm meant to walk it. I need him to come back to me. He will come back, there is no way he would leave me here alone. The doctor says something to Boh and walks out while Bridget follows him. Cash is nowhere to be seen, and Boh is sitting beside the hospital bed, holding Jace's hand with his head cast down.

"Boh," I whisper. Boh looks up at me with bloodshot eyes.

"He will come back to us." I smile.

He forces a smile back at me. I know it's hard to think positively, but I can't think any other way.

"I'm going to get some coffee. Bridge will be back soon. Do you want anything?" Boh stands up, letting go of Jace's hand.

"A coffee would be great."

"Cash said you haven't eaten anything. I will grab you a sandwich, you need to eat and be strong for when he wakes up," he says, looking at Jace with a hint of a hope in his eyes.

"I know. A sandwich would be great, thanks, Boh." Boh nods, heading toward the door.

"Where has Cash gone?" I question before he slips out of the door.

"He just headed out for some fresh air, he will be back soon," he replies before walking out.

Fresh air sounds like a good idea, but I don't want to leave Jace on his own. I'll wait until he's back, then go get some myself. I slip my hand in Jace's and bring it up to my mouth, holding my lips to the back of his hand, the warmth of his skin on my lips calms my racing heart. Ten minutes later, Boh walks back in with a tray of coffees and sandwiches. I grab the coffee straight away, needing to feel a hit of energy.

"Are you okay to stay with Jace, I want to get some fresh air too."

Boh nods. "Of course, Ry. Go get some air, but please eat when you come back." He looks at me with pleading eyes and then picks up another coffee, holding it out to me. "If you see Cash, will you give this to him, he went out the doors just opposite when you walk out of this room."

I smile and nod while taking the second cup of coffee.

"Thanks, Boh."

As I approach the door, a feeling of dread hits me. I turn, looking at Jace. I know he will still be here when I get back, but it feels as though walking out of this door will be the last time I see him. I can't explain the feeling. I walk back to the bed, and Boh looks up at me, and his shoulders sag a little as if he knows what I'm feeling. I don't think I can walk out of the room and not have him beside me.

"Ry, he will still be here when you get back."

I shoot a look to Boh. "I don't know if I can leave him." I keep my eyes on Jace, just walking toward the door made me feel like I lost him briefly.

Boh stands up and walks around to where I'm standing and grabs my face in both hands. "Listen to me," he says, his eyes boring into mine. "Go get some fresh air. Clear your mind, bring that positivity back. He isn't going anywhere. I will come and grab you if the doctor comes back or anything happens, Ry. He needs you fighting fit for when he wakes."

Boh is right, I need to get my strength up. When I'm back, I'll eat and make sure I get some sleep but ask Cash if we can do a sleep routine. I want someone awake at all times. If Jace wakes up, I need someone to be awake and there with him.

I walk toward the door and swing it open. I don't turn around, knowing if I do, I will never leave until he wakes up. I push through the doors Boh mentioned. I'm pretty sure these are fire doors, but no alarms have gone off yet. The air hits me, and I have to admit, it feels good. It feels like a hit of adrenaline, giving me a sliver of energy I have been needing. I glance right and then left, but I don't see Cash. I place the coffees down on the ground and crouch on the pavement, letting my butt hit the concrete.

It's quiet here, it doesn't feel like I'm in the city. Trees surround the back of the hospital. I would assume this is where people come to smoke. I don't even smoke, but I could use one right now. I drop my head back against the wall and close my eyes, letting the light breeze whip around my face. Opening my eyes, I squint up at the bright sun peeking out of the clouds, letting myself, for a moment, feel like everything is perfect. It's not, but it feels good to pretend. Sighing heavily, I stare straight ahead of me, sipping on my coffee. There's sniffling coming from around the corner, so I stand up and walk over there. Cash is kneeled with his head resting in his hands while his shoulders shake uncontrollably.

"Cash," I gently whisper.

He looks up with bloodshot eyes. Kneeling in front of him, I hand him the coffee.

"Cash, it's going to be okay, Jace will be okay." I say it more for myself than him, if I keep telling myself this, it will come true. It has too.

"Rylee," he says with a hint of anger, "stop with your delusional thoughts. Jace is in a coma on life support and the doctor has said himself we need to take each day as it comes. My son could fucking die. Do you understand that? Can you comprehend that? You need to wake up and get in the real world, Rylee. I can't have you around me with all your 'Jace will be fine,' you don't know that!"

He stands up and walks back inside, leaving me in the kneeling position, stunned at his outburst. I sigh, dropping back to the ground. I don't know what he wants me to say. You have to think positive at a time like this. If you don't, then how will you get through the days, how will you keep going, knowing one of the most important people in your life may not come back to you. I pull my phone out of my pocket and pull up Toni's number, if anyone will make me feel better, it will be her. Toni picks up on the first ring.

"Rylee!" she shouts.

"He-ey," I reply, crumbling just from hearing her voice.

I try my hardest to relay everything to Toni through our breaks of crying. I'm trying to stay positive but saying it out loud, repeating what the doctor said is harder than I thought. Toni sniffles on the other end. We stay on the phone in silence for minutes, but it feels like hours, listening to each other cry. Toni never realizes she is my safe space, even sitting with her in silence or on the other end of the phone in silence heals me in a way she will never understand.

"Jace will fight for you, Ry," Toni says, breaking the silence.

"I hope he does. If he doesn't, I don't know how I'm going to get through life, Ton." We fall back into comfortable silence again. There are so many things going around in my head, so many questions I can't ask, that can't be answered. I know Toni will have questions, but she doesn't push or ask, knowing I can't answer them. I just hope when Jace wakes up he can finally explain what's happening and why he took the drugs.

Chapter 17

Bridge was back when I got back to the room. She watched me to ensure I took every bite of the sandwich. I was starving but as soon as I finished it, I felt like I could throw it back up. I managed to keep it down, but I don't think I could handle anything bigger for the time being.

Bridge mentioned I should go home for the night, but I shut that down before she could continue. If I struggled being out of the room for twenty minutes, I can't even imagine how I would feel if I were away for a whole night. I also can't bring myself to tell her I can't bear to step foot in the apartment without Jace. Knowing he won't be there, it won't feel right.

Cash mostly sleeps and barely talks to me when he isn't, which is nothing new, but he's shut himself away from everyone. Bohdi included. He's in his own world, staring at Jace all day. We all are.

I'm sure I've seen his eyes flicker, but I think it's just my hope.

Bridget gives me a kiss on my cheek.

"I'm going to go home, freshen up, and grab you and Cash some more clothes, okay? I will be back a bit later." She smiles as she strokes the top of my head.

Cash is still just staring at Jace. He doesn't even pay Bridge a minute of attention. I smile at her and say, "Thank you." She glances at Cash and then back at me with a tight smile.

Once Bridget has left, we sit in silence, staring at Jace. This would probably be uncomfortable for most people, but I'm used to the silence with Cash. I'm used to him treating me as if I don't exist most of the time. When I realized it was Jace lying in the bed and Cash held me, I was shocked to say the least. Come to think of it, I don't think he has ever hugged me before, but I think that was just an in-the-moment thing. He has sure kept conversation to a minimal since. I don't care though; all I care about is Jace getting better. I just wish Cash would make this ordeal easier by being a normal human for once in his life, and not the moody, rude asshole he is to me. You would at least think he would put aside whatever hate he has mustered up for me while the person we both love more than anything is lying in a fucking coma in a hospital bed. The more I think of it, the angrier it makes me.

Just as I'm about to spew my hate at him, he stands up and walks out. No "*I'll be back in a minute*," or anything. *Fucking asshole.*

I place my hand over Jace's, allowing his warmth to seep into my body, there is nothing in this world that could calm and ground me as much as Jace's touch. I close my eyes, taking in a deep breath and just feeling. Taking in the feel of Jace's skin, the smoothness of it, I glide my fingers through every dip in his hand, then turn his palm over and place my fingers between his, holding his hand. I open my eyes to our joined hands and look up. His face is still wrapped, but they change the dressings every day. At least I can still see glimpses of his beautiful face.

"My beautiful boy," I whisper out. Early hours this morning, when I couldn't sleep, I searched information about comas, and it has been highly suggested you should talk to them. They say they can hear you, and some people have even said it can speed up their recovery process.

"Hey, baby." I get up close to make sure that if the chance is there, he can hear me.

"I miss you so much, Jace. Please come back to us. We all need you right now. Your dad is being an ass." I laugh out. "I know you would be finding an excuse to stick up for him right now and tell me not to take it personally. Even though we know it is personal," I whisper with a smirk.

"Bridge and Boh have been here daily. Just chilling with us. Waiting."

I graze the bit of his cheek that is showing and then rest my hand on his chest.

"I have been inundated with calls and texts from the boys, and hundreds of other people, you won't believe how loved you are. I mean, who can blame them. You're one of the most precious souls I have ever encountered," I say with a lump forming in my throat.

"Please. Please come back to us, Jace. I don't know how long I can stay like this. Without you. I need to feel your touch. I need to see your beautiful blue eyes shining back at me when I walk in the door. I need to hear you calling me your Ry Bear. Please,

Jace. Please." I break out into sobs and rest my forehead on his chest, wishing for a miracle.

"If I could swap places with you, I would do it in a heartbeat. I would take every bit of pain you encountered just to see you smile again." I cry into his chest.

I turn my head, laying my cheek against his chest, facing the door. I open my eyes and am startled seeing Cash standing in the doorway with a collapsed posture, as if he has a weight of grief pushing him down. He looks down at the floor and turns around, walking back out of sight.

I sigh, turning my head and kissing Jace's chest before standing and wiping my tears away. Taking my position back on the chair next to the bed, I hold Jace's hand. As long as I can look at him and touch him, I will hold every bit of faith I have that he will come back to us. He has no choice, he has too. I lay my head down on top of our linked hands and close my eyes. Feeling somewhat content with Jace's hand in mine.

Sometime later, I hear my name being called. I open my eyes and do the first thing I do every time I wake up, I look at Jace, hoping I will see the blue staring back at me. Each time, it never happens, but I hold hope it does one day soon.

"It's just me, Ry," Bridget says.

Bridget is standing there with Boh. I hear voices and peer around Bridget to see Cash talking to a doctor, and it's not the same one as earlier.

"The doctor is here to say they have Jace's results back. He wants to speak with us." Bridget peers into my eyes, giving me a tight-lipped smile that tries to give hopefulness, but her unshed tears that are hovering, waiting to fall, show anything but hope.

I feel better after speaking to Jace earlier. I have all hope this is going to be good news. I can feel it. I get up and straighten my top.

"Okay, lets go." I smile at Bridge while grabbing her hand and walking toward the doctor and Cash. The doctor appears tired. I can't imagine how hard their job must be, and the stress it must cause on them.

"We will talk about Jace's results in another room, please follow me," the doctor says as he turns around and walks out. We follow him and sit down in the next room.

There are two chairs at the front, Cash sits down in one while Bridge and Boh offer the other chair to me. I sit down while Bridge and Boh stand behind us. The doctor offers to go and grab more chairs but they decline. He looks down at papers, then back up to each of us.

"As you are aware, we have been running various tests on Jace."

We were asked to leave the room on a couple of occasions so they could run tests. They had to do physical tests and also wanted to do electronic tests. Cash and I were trying to find out how they went when they let us back in the room, but they wouldn't tell us anything then. They said they needed to wait for some further results.

The doctor's chest rises as he takes a deep breath. "Jace had extreme trauma to his head and was not breathing for a long period of time. This caused significant brain damage."

"Spit it out, doc. What are you trying to say?"

He nods and swallows slightly before saying, "I'm terribly sorry, but there is no activity in Jace's brain." He pauses.

"So, what are you saying exactly?" I say, not understanding.

"Jace is brain dead," he says with a monotone voice. "I'm afraid there is nothing else we can do, the ventilator is the only thing keeping Jace breathing."

I sit in silence. Staring at the doctor. Trying to piece together what he said. *No. I'm dreaming. It's just a nightmare.*

Wake up, Rylee.

"Wake up, Rylee," I say to the room.

"I'm so sorry. I will leave you all alone together. I will be down the hall if you need anything." The doctor walks out of the room, closing the door behind him.

I look down at my hand.

Pinch. Wake up.

Bridge screaming and sobbing fills the room.

Pinch. Wake up.

"My boy. Not my boy," Cash sobs out.

Please wake up. Please.

Bridget has collapsed on the floor, crying into the ground while Bohdi is on his knees between Cash's legs, hugging him while they uncontrollably cry.

I stand up and walk backward, I need to get out of here. It feels like the walls are closing in on me. I turn and run. I run away from the room, from the doom that has pushed me under the waves and is not letting me come up for air. I'm pushing everyone out of my way. I need to come up for air. I slam into the doors, the fresh air hitting my face, the air filling my lungs as I gulp it in. Collapsing to my knees, I stare up at the sky, and time stands still. Everything around me stops.

It's that moment I realize, I'm not asleep, this is real, it's all very real.

My Jace, he's not coming back to me.

Chapter 18

"It feels so good to be back with you, Ry. I missed you so much," Jace whispers into my ear. I hug him tight, I can't believe he is back here. I won't question how he is here with me right now. I'm just so happy he is.

"I thought I lost you," I sob into his chest.

I open my eyes and look to the side where Jace and I are standing. There are flowers everywhere. I lean away from his chest, taking in the scene, and we are standing in a field of flowers. I can't see anything beyond the field. The flowers are all bright colors, and it's then I realize they are tulips. We are standing in a field of different colored tulips, my favorite flower.

He grabs my chin. "Look at me, baby." He sweeps the hair away from my face and grabs me by the cheeks. I get lost in his beautiful blue eyes. I'm so overjoyed to be here with him.

"You can never lose me, Rylee. I will always be here." He drops his hand and points to my heart. "Don't ever forget that, my Ry Bear. You will always own my heart in every way possible. I love you so much."

He bends down and places a ghost of a kiss on my lips. "I love you so much too, Jace," I whisper into his lips, holding onto him for dear life. He brings me close to him and holds onto me tightly. I melt into his arms, content at being surrounded by his smell and his warmth. He hugs me so tightly I feel like I can't breathe, but I don't care. If never breathing again meant seeing Jace, I would take my last breath right now. I don't ever want Jace to let me go. I look up at him, and there's tears glistening his eyes. Panic fills me. I go to ask what's wrong, but Jace puts his finger over my mouth.

"Don't ever forget, Ry. It's us. Always. Forever."

I open my eyes, and Jace is lying there, and I sob out, realizing seeing him was in my dream. *Did he come to me in my dream?* Realization hits me over what has happened in the last twenty-four hours.

"Nooooooo," I scream out on a sob. I can't hold it in, the sickness that fills my stomach hits me. I can't believe my world has given up on us, on me. I'm leaning over myself, holding my stomach, everything hurts. Arms wrap around me from behind.

"I got you, Ry," Boh whispers in my ear. Boh crouches down and holds onto me. I know I should be consoling him, but I can't, I selfishly can't think about anyone else right now. All I can think is I will never see those ocean-blue eyes staring at me again. I'll never see the big glowing smile grace his face when he walks in from work and sees me. The way his eyes wrinkle when he smiles so big just because he's happy to see my face. The way he calls me Ry Bear when he wants something. Or even his smell . . . Jace's smell. I cry uncontrollably into Boh, this doesn't feel real. *How can this be real?*

Boh holds me tighter, shaking while crying into my hair. I sit up slightly, and Boh loosens his hold on me while he looks at me. The grief and sadness I feel is shining back at me through his eyes. Blotchy marks cover his face. I stare into his eyes, and they are covered with red lines, and for a moment, they remind me of Jace's, but they will never be my Jace's. No one will ever be Jace.

"Please, tell me it's all a dream, Boh. Please," I plead, holding onto my stomach.

Boh can't even speak, he just drops his head, crying, and shakes it side to side. I pull myself out of Boh's hold and stand up, getting closer to the bed. I sit beside Jace, getting as close as I can so I can touch him. I wrap his hand in mine, and I expect it to be cold, but it's not, its warm, like he always is. I let this ground me for all of five seconds before reality crashes down on me again. I lay my head on his chest, feeling it rise and fall. He's breathing, they don't know what they are talking about. I squeeze my eyes closed, drowning in the feel of his chest moving. I let myself live in a world where it's him breathing, not the machine. It's Jace, he is breathing on his own, and soon he will wake up and be better and come home with me.

"Please wake up, Jace. Please," I whisper into his chest.

I hear a scoff and then a loud laugh behind me. This breaks me out of my dream where Jace will wake up and come back home. The pain hits my chest like a truck, and I sit up, turning around in slow motion, as if I have weights holding me down. Cash is standing by the door . He wasn't there before, I don't think. Although, I wasn't paying attention to anything other than Jace. Cash is still laughing in a satanic way.

"Here she goes again." He smirks at me, but I can see the pain in his eyes, the sadness he is drowning in.

"*Please wake up, Jace*," he mimics me in a little girl voice. He shakes his head side to side, and his stare hits me like a knife to the chest.

"Either you step back into reality and understand my son is not coming back. Or"—he points at me, stalking closer—"you"—he takes another step—"can"—and another step—"get"—now he's standing only centimeters away from me—"the fuck out!" he roars in my face.

I shrink back into Jace's side because it makes me feel like he's by my side, sticking up for me. I raise my chin. "Fuck you!"

Boh grabs Cash by his shoulder and pulls him in for a hug. Cash breaks down into Boh's shoulders. His knuckles turn white from gripping Boh like he is the only thing holding him up. I'm not taking it personal like I normally do, in this moment, I think of someone else; what it must feel like to lose a son.

I know Cash is hurting, so I turn back around and lie next to Jace, avoiding all the wires and tubes, and get as close to him as I can. I need to be near him to feel him. Closing my eyes, it's like nothing has changed, I'm lying next to Jace back at our apartment in bed on a Sunday morning. If I open my eyes, I'll see him emailing away on his phone, or looking at the latest stats for his favorite soccer team. It's where I am in my head, and it's that moment I sit there thinking back to those times; they were the most simplest things but I then realize they are my favorite moments. Jace and I closed away from the world, just us.

I hear voices around me. Bridget. I don't want to open my eyes, all the time I have them closed and my head laying near Jace, feeling the movement of his chest, I'm in a happy place. I can breathe when I'm here with him, he makes my world clear of any void or sadness. He is my happy place, he has been since he entered in my life. I don't know how I went twenty years without him in it, everything before meant nothing to me once I met him. My life started that night at Freedom, the night he bumped into me and I stared into his perfect eyes. My life roared to life in that moment.

I squeeze his arm and let reality crawl its way into my mind and sob into him. I cry for him and wish I could take it all away and pass it on to me. I open my eyes, and I turn his wrist around to see the *R*. As I run my fingers across it, a small smile graces my lips at the memory of us getting the matching tattoos done. Thinking back to our two-year anniversary and the way he begged me to let him get my name tattoed on him. I begged him not to, not because I didn't want him to, but I just didn't want him regretting it. Now, I know he would never, but at the time, I was still unsure on how he truly felt for me. Now, I have no doubt he loves me.

Or loved me . . . As I think of having to use that in past tense, the stabbing pain in my heart increases. I remember him pleading and begging me with those eyes, and there is no saying no to those eyes, so I compromised and said he could get an R and I would get a J. I knew how I felt for Jace then, I was head over heels and couldn't picture my life without him, he was it for me. I would have happily had "Jace" tattooed on me, but I knew he would then get Rylee, so I settled for the J too.

Leaving the memory, I look back down at the J as tears pour out of my eyes. I wish now we both got our full names. I stare at the blurry J through the tears in my eyes. We always spoke about getting our kids' names tattooed and what we would have. He said he wanted their names going up his arm above the R but in smaller writing. The thought of never having children with the other half of me. I always wondered what it would be like to see my children and realize I made them with the person I love most in this world—two halves with one half being so amazingly perfect. This crushes me like nothing else, I will never get that future we nonstop spoke about, it was taken from me before it could ever truly begin. I wail into Jace's side, letting everything out, there is no pain out there like this, and I don't know how I'm going to do this without him.

I hear Bridget before I see her.

"Rylee, wake up." Bridget's hand rests on my shoulder.

I open my eyes, and I have wrapped myself up with Jace and am holding him tighter than I ever have before. *Did I never hold him tight enough*? I don't ever remember holding him this tight. I hope he knows I loved holding him. My mind races 100 mph, thinking about everything and wondering if Jace knew how much I loved him. *Did I show him how much?* I feel like my mind is blanking out, and this sends me into a shock of panic. *Why can't I remember him, remember our memories?* I shoot up, and Bridget is telling me to calm down.

"Did he know how much I love him?" I cry out frantically.

Bridget has tears in her eyes.

"Jace knew you loved him more than life, Rylee. Not even just Jace, everyone knew that by the way you looked at him—like he hung the moon and the stars, Rylee. Jace knew every inch of your feelings, never doubt that."

I fall onto Bridget's chest. "I'm sorry, my mind is blank, I feel like I'm forgetting him already, Bridge."

Bridget brings me in for a cuddle and we stand there crying into each other, holding each other up. She's leaning on me as much as I am her. There's a knock, so I glance over Bridget's shoulder and see the doctor standing there from yesterday.

"Ms. Matthews. Ms Stiles." Cash and Boh are nowhere to be seen.

"Yes," I say, standing back from Bridget and wiping my eyes and nose on my sleeve.

"We have another doctor coming in later, I will come back with him, but it would be good if we could have a chat when he arrives, if this is okay with you?"

Bridget and I nod.

"Thank you. If there is anything I or the other staff can do, please do let one of us know." He gives us a tight smile.

"Thanks, doctor."

When he leaves, I look over at Jace, my eyes gravitating to his chest: up, down, up down. This makes me breathe easier. I know it's crazy, but it's like he is still here with us. I drag my eyes to the tubes and then at the machine, then to Bridget, and as if she knows what I'm thinking, tears pour from our eyes again. We know what this meeting will be regarding, but none of us will ever be ready to hear those words.

Chapter 19

We all gather in the room that made our worlds come crashing down only yesterday. Bridge had to call Boh to find out where they were, she didn't tell me, but to be honest, I don't care. I'm numb right now. It feels like I'm in limbo, and even though I know what is going on and what is happening, my brain is struggling to keep up with it.

"I would ask how you are all doing but I know that will be a silly question," the doctor starts off.

Everyone just stays silent because what are you meant to say to that. *Yes, doctor that would be.* We're staring at him, waiting to see what he will say, even though we all know deep down what the inevitable is.

"Following on from yesterday . . ." He pauses, looking at each of us, it's like you can feel the impending doom just from his gaze.

"We need to speak about when you would like to turn Jace's machine off."

I don't say anything. *How can I tell someone to turn my boyfriend's breathing machine off? How can I tell someone when I will be okay with that?* I will never be okay with it. Never will I be okay with not seeing or speaking to the person I love most in this world again.

No one speaks, Bridget looks down at the floor while crying. Cash stares at a spot on the floor, not saying a word. Boh scans me with tears in his eyes, helpless and not knowing what to do. Me? I just stand here, numb. No tears, no feelings. Nothing. *When did this happen?* Everyone stays silent, and as much as I'm numb, I still don't think I can bring myself to speak. I don't know what I would say. Beg them not to turn it off, pray for a miracle and hope his brain miraculously starts working again. The doctor continues looking between us and then places his hands together on the table.

"I know this must be hard for you, but—"

"Have you got a son?" Cash asks, narrowing his eyes at the doctor, the blackness and large bags under them are proof of the lack of sleep and constant crying.

As if the doctor has had this question asked to him a dozen times, he simply shakes his head at Cash and calmly states, "No, Mr. Stiles. I don't."

"So that question you just asked, you don't know how that feels, then, do you?" Cash says with a bite to his tone.

"No, I don't. I have all sympathy—"

"Then you cannot sit there and ask such a question as if we are expected to tell you," he spits, staring back at the spot he was staring at before.

"I will give you some more time, but this is something you need to think about." The doctor rushes out before Cash can bite anything back. We are all now just sitting in silence. Boh is the first to speak up.

"I . . . I guess I should call around and—" He can't even finish before he breaks out in a sob.

Bridge walks over to him, crying while Cash stands and leaves the room in angry strides.

I walk out and head back to Jace's room. I would rather spend all the time I can with him. I don't know what is wrong with me and why everything has gone numb.

I lean up against the door in Jace's room, staring at him, watching his chest rise and fall.

I know what Boh meant when he said he will ring round. He is going to ring people to come say their goodbyes. How, I don't know, Jace is loved by everyone. He would have people lined up out the doors. No one has been to visit him. We just didn't want people seeing him like this, and we knew Jace wouldn't have wanted that, but what are we to do now. We have no choice. That decision was taken out of our hands.

This will be the last image of Jace in their heads. Bandages wrapped around his beautiful face. Wires coming out of his body. A fucking machine breathing for him. It's not Jace at all. It's not our Jace. The worst thing is they won't see that big infectious smile that would light up a whole room and those blue eyes shining like the biggest star. People gravitate toward Jace, and I don't blame them. He draws people in and then they don't want to leave, they don't not want to know Jace. His personality is as infectious as him. He is the most amazing person I have ever met. Now the world is going to take that from us.

I blink open my eyes to see Rowan standing there staring at Jace with tears trickling down his face. I move my arm which makes his eyes clash with mine. Rowan has been Jace's best friend since they were kids, they were inseparable, he had the pleasure of watching Jace grow up.

"How did this happen, Ry. I can't say goodbye to him," he sobs out while his shoulders shake. He brings his hands to his face and cries loud into them. I stand up, walk over to him, and embrace him. Letting our grief and hurt support each other. We stand there for what feels like an eternity. Our tears dry up and we just stand there staring at Jace.

I kiss Rowan on the cheek and tell him I will give him time. I walk out, not being able to see anyone say their goodbyes. I don't know how I'm going to do it, but there is no way I can watch anyone else. I walk out the fire escape door, needing some fresh air and silence. Cash is standing there staring at nothing in particular and doesn't even hear me walk up beside him. We just stand there in silence. He knows I'm standing here, but we just let the slight breeze lap against our face. The fresh air makes you feel a little lighter, it's like the hospital is a cage and being out here is freedom. That's when Cash brings a cigarette to his mouth. I have never seen him smoke before, I'm pretty sure he doesn't smoke but if anything would make someone start the up the habit, this is it. I'm not about to address the cigarette, I don't blame him.

"You know, as a child, Jace always had the tendency to make people smile with just a look," Cash says, still staring ahead. I stand there in complete silence, wanting to know everything about Jace as child. I'm jealous that I wasn't there, that I didn't know him through most of his life.

"The big blue eyes he has, they were even more pronounced as a child. With his small little round face and a smile that would light up the whole solar system." Cash clears his throat, taking a long pull from the white stick.

"He was even the perfect baby. You wouldn't hear a murmur out of him, then the minute you would go check on him he would just lie there, looking at you with the biggest smile on his face. He was such a happy baby, child, and adult." Cash has tears sliding down his cheeks, one by one. I don't know if he would want me to comfort him. We rarely communicate, so I don't really know how to act with him now.

"Sorry," he rushes out, wiping his face with his arm.

"Don't be sorry, Cash. You have nothing to be sorry about." I lay my hand on his arm, which causes him to flinch while his shoulders hunch up. I don't remove it because I think this is what Cash needs. Someone to just be here and listen, it's what we all need. His shoulders slowly relax. I run my hand up and down his arm, wanting him to continue talking about Jace. I want to know every minute of every day of Jace's life, it will make me feel like I haven't missed out if I know everything.

"Even now, Rylee, I look at him and think, how did I get so lucky to have such an amazing son. How did an asshole like me end up with him?" He studies me as if I have the answer, and to be honest, I don't because I have wondered the exact same thing, multiple times.

"He definitely got his hardworking genes from you, Cash," I say, hoping this will make him feel even an inch better.

"I wouldn't say that is a good thing, Rylee. He always worked too much, just like me. I even asked him to stop doing the hours he was doing, but he never listened. He loved his job and what he did." Cash looks down at the ground. "I just wish he had done more in life instead of dedicating so much to work," he whispers, still staring at the floor. The cigarette he is holding is burning down, nearly to his fingers. I grab it out of his hand and throw it on the ground, stamping on it. I pick it up and walk over to the bin. When I walk back to Cash, he's staring straight at me for the first time since being out here.

"I'm sorry, Ry. I'm really sorry for the way I have acted since being here," he says with pain in his eyes.

It's not an apology for all the times before, but I don't care. I don't have the energy to argue with him anymore and have that constant tension floating around the room every time we are left alone together. We all need each other now, and I know for certain I need him, Boh, and Bridge more than they could ever imagine.

"It's okay." I'm not going to say it's justified or not to worry about it because he has made things harder for not just me but all of us since being here. Now is not the time to bring this up, though. Cash stares at me a second longer, huffing and looking down.

"It's not, but thank you for being nice about it." He continues staring at the floor. "You know . . ." he says, pausing for a moment like he's struggling how to say the next words he wants too. ". . . he loved you like you wouldn't believe, Rylee. He spoke about you nonstop at work."

I didn't expect those words, and they hit me like a truck going 100 mph. The pain laces through my veins like poison, stinging my already aching heart. I knew Jace loved me, I was confident in that, he told me every chance he could but hearing this come from someone else, someone like his dad, it kills me. I literally feel like someone is cutting into my chest and tearing my heart from it. Knowing he won't be able to tell people he loves me or talk about me again triggers something in me, and even though it's killing me, I can't stop the next words.

"Tell me more," I say on a small whisper. I'm trying not to break down in front of Cash, but I'm finding it hard holding it in right now. I want to know what he said about me when he wasn't with me, and I want someone to tell me how much he loves me. I want to hear it come out of people's mouths forever.

"It was rare I would see him walk in work without a smile on his face." He smiles lightly, looking at me from the side and then up at the sky.

"Yes, he was a happy person, but not always, Rylee. He did go through some times in his life, not long before he met you." Jace has said odd things about me bringing light into his life when he couldn't see any. I never questioned it; I was just happy I made him happy.

"Why was he not happy before?" I want to know more about how much he loves me, but I want to know what also made him sad before me. I want to know it all.

He takes a big sigh, his shoulders raising until he drops them.

"I think it was his mom." I am startled to hear this. I knew little about Jace's mom as he barely knew anything himself. He told me she left him and Cash when he was just one. It broke my heart when he told me, but he always acted as if he didn't care. He always said, "How can you care about someone who you never knew or even remember."

"Jace always acted as if he didn't care about her?"

"I don't think he did." He pauses. "Most of the time."

Cash reaches into his pocket to pull out another cigarette and lights it. He peers at the ground, kicking tiny stones with his foot.

"He went through a stage, wanting to find her and see why she left. It was a hard time because there is no way she deserved Jace in her life. She was an awful person, and I knew if, and that was a big if, Jace found her, she would hold onto him like a leech and probably bleed him dry. She wasn't a mother, she was a piece of trash. I didn't want Jace searching for her and thinking he wasn't good enough, so I told him the truth about her."

"What was the truth?" I say, trying to show my eagerness of wanting to know.

"She was a deadbeat, druggy prostitute," he deadpans.

Chapter 20

My eyes go wide. I never expected Cash to come out with that. Also, I can't help but think Cash and a prostitute just doesn't make sense. He is so clean cut and just Cash.

"I . . . I. That's a shock," I admit.

Cash nods. "Only family know the truth about her. I was a rebel when I was younger, believe it or not," he says with a slight smirk. "And stupidly fell in love with a girl who I thought loved me too. Little did I know, she was a money-grabbing whore." He laughs but it's a sad laugh.

I don't know what to say to this. No wonder Jace never told me, he must have been ashamed. I wish he had told me. I would have been there for him.

"When she found out she was pregnant, it was quite late into the pregnancy. She was traumatized, saying she was going to get rid of the baby. I told her over my dead body and that we would raise the baby together. I was over the moon, the girl I loved was pregnant with my baby. What more could a guy want? It soon all came crashing down when she went into a fit of rage and told me why she couldn't have the baby. She screamed how it would lose her money and how she couldn't get through the pregnancy without the drugs." He laughs.

"I was confused at first what she meant about losing money. It's then she told me everything," he says, staring at the ground.

"I went and told my parents everything, and at the time, I was heartbroken and scared for my unborn child. They were angry, very angry, but thankfully, they didn't want her getting an abortion either. I managed to talk her into having the baby and staying off the drugs. She was on twenty-four-hour watch by me and my family. The withdrawals were pretty bad, but she got through it with our help."

I stay in silence, wanting Cash to finish.

"The day her water broke, I can't tell you how happy I was." He smiles bright this time. Like he can see the memories in front of him.

"When Jace was born, the moment I laid eyes on him, I knew what real love was. I knew from that moment I would cherish and love him more than anyone ever could. He was so perfect. Content and fat." He laughs out the last word.

"Ten pounds, eight ounces. Jace's mom was in bits of course, but I was ecstatic. I wanted to scream it from the highest mountain that I was a dad." His smile falls as his head drops.

"The following weeks, months were the happiest I had ever been, but I knew Jace's mom was back on the drugs, and I also knew she was back out there, sleeping around for money. Weird enough, it was like I didn't care. She kept attempting to see him while being high as a kite most of the time. It was weird I never noticed how high she was previously, it is true what they say 'love is blind' because she was an angel in my eyes. Full of purity.

"When I found out about the drugs and prostitution when she was pregnant, it was like the blindfold was finally lifted and I could see her for what she was. She did hide it well from me, but after she told me, she stopped applying the heavy makeup and trying to make herself look like someone she wasn't. She no longer looked angelic, no longer dressed in her cute summer dresses, and instead she would wear miniskirts with tiny crop tops, she stopped applying the concealer to her track-covered arms. She was the devil in disguise, but she gave me a meaning to life, she gave me Jace, and he triggered something in me the day he was born. No one else mattered except him, and I promised myself I would do anything and everything to keep him safe," he sobs out the last sentence.

"I couldn't even do that." Tears pour from Cash's eyes. His shoulders crumple as he cries and cries into his hands.

On instinct, I grab Cash and hug him as best as I can. With how big he is, compared to me, it's hard, but I know he needs to lean on someone now, and I want to be that someone. We cry together, cry for Cash losing the son he cherished more than anything, and cry for me, for losing the one person that meant everything to me. We cry until we can't cry anymore. Cash slowly pulls away from me.

"I didn't mean to break down on you like that. Just the memories of seeing him come into this world, I never thought I would be around to see him leave it."

Talking to Cash was a little escape of reality, it didn't take my mind off things, as everything was still based around Jace, but it just felt like we were having a casual chat. It didn't feel like we were talking about someone who won't be on this earth for much longer. Cash saying he never thought he would see Jace leave this world brings everything crashing back. I feel like a huge weight has been placed back on my shoulders. My body is slowly breaking down again.

I glance at the doors and then back at Cash, silently telling him we need to go back in there, back in the cage, the doom of what we don't want to come. He nods and we both go to step but then Cash reaches out and grabs my arms, stopping me. I turn around and look at him.

"There was a point to me telling you all that, Rylee. I want you to know how after me telling Jace everything about his mom, he went into a dark place. Then you came along and brought him out of that dark place and made him the happiest he has ever been." A ghost of a smile graces his lips.

"I want you to know, I'm thankful for you being in his life, Rylee. You brought my son back to us and made him see that not all women are like his mom. He loved you more than anyone on this earth. I just wanted you to know that," he whispers and walks past me, opening the door, waiting for me to walk in. I raise my hand, signaling one minute to him. He nods, letting go of the door and disappearing from my sight.

I stand there unable to move, unable to do anything. The weight of everything once again comes crashing down on me like a boulder. Smashing me into pieces. I stare at the door, thinking back to what Cash said about me bringing Jace back. "I might have brought him back to you then, but I can't now . . ."

Chapter 21

The day has passed in a blur. Not long after coming back in, Cash wanted to speak with us all. What came out of his mouth, crushed my soul. Everything around me spun when I heard the words, "We can't keep holding on to hope when there is none. I keep thinking what Jace would want, and he wouldn't want this. He wouldn't want us to keep praying for hope and sitting around the bed watching a machine breathe for him. We need to let him go. I want to tell the doctors to turn the machine off tonight. I just want us four there with him, no one else." He spoke the words like he had rehearsed them a million times, and he probably had in his head. In my head, I was screaming no, but I had to agree, Jace wouldn't want any of this.

People have come and gone, and I have stayed clear of the room or even speaking to anyone. I need this time to myself. I haven't been able to eat anything all day. This is like nothing I have ever felt, it's like the gates of hell are only around the corner and I'm heading straight for them. I'm sitting in a quiet waiting room, and luckily no one has been in here today. It has just been me and my thoughts. Memories of Jace, and all the fun times we had.

In a way it's like my whole life has flashed before my eyes, knowing that as of tonight, my Jace will no longer be with us. I keep wondering how I am taking this so well. Over the last week, I had my days, but deep down, I always knew this was coming. It doesn't make it easier, but my mind is lagging, having trouble catching up with the present. My heart is in the present, it hurts so much, the ache I constantly have, and the emptiness, it's like I have turned hollow. I thought sitting in this room today would make my day go slow, drag out the inevitable, but it hasn't. I have been so caught up in my feelings that it flew by.

There is a knock at the door, and the minute I see the doctor's face, I know it's time. My stomach sinks, as if it's dropping into hell, waiting for me to come get it, and where Jace is, is the room to hell. This is it. I told Cash, Bridget, and Boh earlier today I didn't want to be in the room when they said their goodbyes. I want to do mine on my own. Being in there with them would be too much.

As I walk out of the room into the hallway, Bridget and Boh are cuddled up on the chair outside Jace's room, sobbing into each other. Cash is nowhere to be seen but then walks out of the room, looking straight at me. He pushes his lips together, trying to give me a tight smile, but smiling is impossible at this moment.

I walk up to Cash. "Have you . . ." I look down, not finishing the sentence, but Cash must know what I mean.

"Not yet, I'm going to go in last, if that's okay. They said we can all be in there together when they do it." He points to the door and walks away, he can't bring himself to say it, and I don't blame him. I can't either. I stare at the door and imagine it black with flames coming out of it. Associating a room that Jace is in like hell is probably not the norm but it's literally how I feel. Saying goodbye to Jace has to be what utter and complete hell would feel like, and I don't want to be anywhere near it. I take a deep breath, putting my hand on the handle. I close my eyes, counting to ten. *You can do this, Rylee.* Bridget and Boh crying behind me sends me forward. I have to do this, I will regret it for the rest of my life if I don't.

The room is so silent, and it doesn't have the feel it did before, although I hated seeing Jace like this, being near him made me calmer. Now my heart is racing so fast I could pass out. My mind is running 1000 mph. *Where do I even start, what do I say?*

I walk up to the bed, bringing my hand up to his face, which is slightly uncovered now. It has cuts and scabs all over the visible part, but it's like they wanted us to be able to see more of him. I touch the areas not harmed, his skin is smooth. I let my fingers trace down to his lips. I brush them along, I always loved his full lips. It was one of the first things I noticed about him.

"Hey, babe."

Is this really goodbye? Am I actually doing this? I never in my life thought I would have to say goodbye to Jace.

"I really don't know what to say, Jace. I always thought you were going to wake up and come back to me, never in a million years did I ever see myself standing here having to do this." There is a small gap next to him I know I'll be able to fit into. I squeeze in and lie on my side, pretending we are lying in bed at home. I lay my hand on his chest, reveling in the rise and fall.

"I love you so, so much. There are no words to describe how I feel for you." I take a minute, gathering my thoughts.

"I knew from the moment I saw you, I was yours. I was always waiting for the other half to me, and I just knew deep down you were it after that night. I'm so thankful I got to meet you and got to share six years with you. It was such an honor to have been loved by you. You gave love a meaning, you are the meaning, the definition of it." Tears fall down my face as I try and hold myself together.

"You will never be forgotten, Jace. I will think about you every second of every day. I don't know if life is worth living without you now that I know what life is like with you. I can't imagine it, but I keep thinking what you would want, and I know you would want me to live. You told me so. I will, Jace. It might take me a while to get there, but I promise you, I will. I have so many unanswered questions, but I'm not going to dwell on them because I will never know the reason. I will never know why this happened but what I do know is"—I bring his arm up to my chest and hold it across my heart—"you will always live in here," I say, thinking back to what he told me in my dream.

I lay my head down, cuddling into him, letting the tears fall down the side of my face onto his chest.

"You took my heart and now you've left it in pieces. If my love could have saved you, you would have lived forever." The weight of everything comes crashing down on me, and I slide out of the bed, drop to the floor, and scream. Everything I have held in today and yesterday, it all comes out. Life is so unfair, I'm so crushed, this agony is unbearable, and it won't stop. I don't think it ever will. I shouldn't be here saying goodbye to the love of my life.

Cash rushes in and drops down next to me, cradling me to his chest. "Shh, shh, I got you, Rylee."

"Let it out," he whispers, and I do, I let it out onto Cash. I cry and scream until I can't cry anymore and my voice is croaky. I know Cash hasn't said his goodbye yet. So I sit up and lean back.

"I'm sorry, I shouldn't have done that, you haven't yet." It's me who can't say it this time. I stand, turning around to Jace, knowing I will be back in here soon to see him take his last breath. I put my hand on Cash's arm and then exit the room. Boh and Bridget are still sitting on the chairs, and seeing me sends tears trickling out of their eyes again. I sit between them, and we all hold each other, not saying a word, just sitting with each other and holding each other up.

I realize we have been sitting here for quite a while, so I stand, thinking I should check in on Cash. I hover by the door, turning to Boh and Bridget.

"Should I check on him?" I whisper.

Bridget shrugs and Boh nods, and they look like they have the weight of the world on their shoulders. I push the handle down slowly and push the door open as quietly as I can. I peek my head around and my eyes well up again. Cash is lying next to

Jace on the opposite side to where I was, one foot still on the floor, keeping him on the bed. He has Jace in the tightest hug he can manage and is crying into his neck. His shoulders violently shaking. I stand there not knowing if I should walk over or leave him. The words that come out of his mouth make my decision for me.

"Save me a space in heaven, my boy," Cash croaks out. I walk over to the bed and rest my hand on Cash's. His back is to me, but he brings his hand up from beside him and places it over mine, squeezing it like he also needs the support he gave me. I rest my face on Cash's shoulder, and we just lie there in silence.

Cash breaks the silence. "We need to do this, Rylee, we need to let him go."

"I know."

I don't make any attempt to move and neither does Cash.

After a while, he moves, so I lift my head off his shoulder and step back. I stare at him, and he nods while bringing me in for a hug.

"Let me go and get Boh and Bridge," I say as I peel myself away from him.

"I'll go get the doctor," he whispers.

Both doctors enter the room, standing to the side, waiting for one of us to say something or give them the sign we are ready. When Cash nods to one of them, they walk around the bed, but my eyes stay on Jace the whole time. Panic fills me as I rush over and plant one last kiss on his forehead, not wanting to ever forget the feel of his skin on my lips.

"Until we meet again, my beautiful boy. Don't be a stranger, come back and visit me in my dreams, Jace," I whisper as close to Jace's ear as I can, in the hope that with some kind of miracle, he can hear me. The tears cascade down my face as I walk back to stand between Bridge and Cash, struggling to keep myself upright, the weight of what is happening has always been there but now it's at its heaviest. We all stand in a line at the end of the bed, waiting.

"Can I ask you to leave the room, while we remove the tubes. I will come and get you once the tubes are removed," the doctor gently asks. I stand there rooted to the spot, not taking my eyes off Jace. I look at Cash with desperation. "Please, Cash. We can't do this. We can't turn those machines off."

"Rylee, don't make this harder than it needs to be," Cash begs. I glance over at Jace, everything collapsing around me. Cash slowly pulls me back as sobs come from him. I don't want to make this harder but how can I let him go. Cash drags me back and then Jace is no longer in sight, the door is closed in front of me as I drop to the floor, as if my world has been ripped away from me in a blink of an eye. I slam my hands on the floor, screaming for Jace while Bridget crouches down, holding me while we cry with each other.

Minutes later, the doctor comes out of the room, signaling for us to enter. My body moves on autopilot. We all stop in a line, waiting with bated breath, staring at Jace. He seems so at peace. I approach Jace with a sense of tranquility. I have seen him like this hundreds of times.

I gaze over his face and then down to his chest. I freeze as a sob escapes me. "His chest," I cry out. "It's not moving." The silence crashes into the room, the machine is no longer beeping, the machine is no longer breathing for him. The silence takes us out one by one. Everything in my life, in my soul stops along with him. Looking at the love of my life, the pain is like nothing I have ever felt before. He's gone, and he's not coming back. I stand there, staring at him and crumble as I realize this will be the last time I say this to Jace's face. "I will love you. Always. Forever."

They say a heart will break but it still keeps beating. I wish mine didn't.

Chapter 22

My phone has been ringing nonstop for three days now. The names and numbers are all blurring together. I know Toni has been ringing me the most. She has been knocking on my apartment door too, shouting through, telling me she has left stuff outside since I won't answer. I don't collect whatever it is. I know she is worried about me, but I don't have the energy to care, in all honesty.

The numbness wore off. My whole body aches, and I'm either lying here staring at the ceiling with no thoughts other than Jace, drowning myself in tears, or I'm smashing up everything in sight that reminds me of him. I'm angry and sad, all in one. I keep praying he will come back to me in my dreams and tell me he loves me, but he doesn't. *Why won't he come back?*

I can't stop sleeping because I get a buzz knowing I'm going to fall asleep and that I might feel his touch and see his blue eyes staring back at me with that big bright smile on his face. He doesn't though. I turn around, letting the silent tears fall from my eyes and soak into the pillow. The pillow is constantly wet from my tears. I haven't changed them since Jace slept in them last, and I can't bring myself to. His smell is fading, shattering the little fragments of what is left of my heart every time I try and chase it. I can't move anything of his, and I keep praying I will wake up and he'll be walking through the door. I know it won't happen, I know, but I just can't stop wishing and hoping.

The pinging noise on my phone starts again. I know I can't keep ignoring people, but I don't want to speak to anyone. *Why can't I just be left alone.* It's Toni again. I love her, I really do but the thought of even having to talk to someone makes my head feel heavier. It's too much energy, too much faking I'm okay when I'm not. The minute you say, "*I'm not okay*," they want to help, but they can't. There is nothing they can do.

My other half, my world, has been taken from me and is not returning. What can they really do? Nothing. I take a deep breath, roll onto my back, and answer the phone. I know she just needs to hear my voice. I know what she's thinking, she's a worrier and always imagines the worst, so I have sent her a couple of texts with an "*xo*" just so she knows I'm okay and I'm just having time to myself and don't want to talk. She is a precious soul. I know she just wants to hear my voice. She has been my rock through a lot of stuff, so the least I can do is answer her phone call.

"Hey," I croak out, realizing I haven't drank any water in a while and my throat hurts a lot.

"Hey, my precious girl," she whispers. I don't say anything else. There isn't really anything to say, I can't engage in normal conversation because I don't care what is going on in the world or in other people's lives. As selfish as it sounds, I don't care at all.

"Can I come around and see you?"

"No." She doesn't say anything.

"I'm sorry, Ton, I just can't. I can't do it. I can't see people and try and act like everything is okay when it's not. I tried so hard when Mom died to be strong, and I did it. I could have got an Oscar for how I acted around people when Mom died. I made out I was fine when I wasn't. I cried myself to sleep for nights, Ton. I'm not doing that again, I can't. Not with Jace." My voice is now raised with tears pouring out of my eyes. As if that was sitting on my chest, I burst out sobbing down the phone to Toni, and she does exactly what I want her to do. She just listens. She lets me sob my heart out.

"I want you to do me a favor, Ry," she cries out.

"What?" I mumble.

"I want you to reach into your pocket for me." At first, I frown, then I realize.

"I want you to take a kiss out, you know the ones we save for when we need them most. This is that time, Ry."

I nod while silently crying. This is the time, this is why we started doing this. I reach into my pj pocket and pull out one of our air kisses.

"I have it," I choke out.

"Hold it to your face."

I hold my hand to my cheek and press into it, holding it there and not letting go.

"Remember a few months back when Jace was laughing at us doing the air kisses like he always does." She pauses, waiting for me to tell her I remember.

"Yes." We were in the kitchen and Toni was getting ready to leave, and before walking out, she turned around and said, "Love ya," blowing a kiss and watching me catch it. Toni looked over my shoulder and smiled before I turned around, and Jace was very obviously trying to hold a laugh in. Then he burst out laughing, saying sorry but it makes him laugh every time. I clearly pouted at him which made him stop laughing and said if he ever blew me a kiss, I better catch it. At that moment, he blew me one and I caught it and put it in my pocket. He asked why I didn't use it there and then, and I told him I would save it for a day I needed it. Dragging myself out of that memory, the tears are falling like a waterfall down my face.

"This is the kiss, Rylee. The kiss you are holding to your face now is the kiss that Jace blew you that day, the one you said you will hold until you need it," she sobs out.

My shoulders shake as the tsunami of tears flow. I cry my heart out, still holding my hand to my face. This is the kiss I needed. I tell myself I can feel his lips touching my cheek and imprinting on me. I don't want to pull my hand away because I know I will lose that feeling, the feeling that Jace is right next to me, holding his lips to my cheek.

"Thank you, Toni. Thank you so much," I cry out to her.

"Don't thank me, Rylee. Just promise me you won't ever give up. Please. I need you as much as you need me. I'm not doing life without you in it."

"I won't give up," I softly say to her, "I promise."

"I love you, Ry."

"I love you too, Ton." We stay on the phone in silence. She listened to me cry, which is what I needed, but she also gave me something even more. Jace's kiss. I know some people will say it's not a kiss. To them, no, but it has always worked for us on our worst days. Knowing I have had Jace's kiss makes my chest feel a little lighter. No, it won't last, but it is nice for now.

I turn over, holding the phone to my ear while Toni lightly sings on the other end, it's quiet enough to know she is singing to herself, but it lulls me into a sense of comfort. I know it will send me into a deep sleep any minute. The thought of seeing Jace's face after the kiss makes a ghost of a smile grace my lips. I might see him once I close my eyes. *I can only wish.*

I wake up a while later with a throbbing headache, which I can only assume was a concoction of all the crying and no hydration. I stretch a little, feeling how much my body aches. I slowly sit up, as I'm slightly dizzy. My shoulders slump as if my body is begging me to lie back down, but I need to get a drink. I head to the kitchen with my blinders on. I don't want all the reminders kicking me in the face at every turn. *As if I can escape the reminders, Jace is in my head every minute of the day.* I grab a cold bottle of water out of the fridge, all the food in there has no doubt gone bad, but I have no energy to sort any of it out. It can rot for all I care. My stomach growls at the thought of food. Even though my body is calling out for it, I dry heave. I drag myself back to bed. I have more missed calls and texts. One of the last text messages was from Toni.

> Toni: Sleep tight, angel. Just drop me a little message each day to let me know you're okay, please. I will give you this week, but I will be around to see you next week, Ry. Even if I have to drive to Cash's and get the spare key.

At least she is giving me the rest of this week. I don't even know what the day is, let alone how far into the week I am. I notice a missed call from Cash, which is odd. We haven't spoken since that day everyone's world came crashing down. Bridge keeps ringing and texting, and I send her the same as I sent Toni. I know they are all grieving and hurting, and I just don't know if us all grieving together is the best thing, well, for me it's not. I then see a text from Cash. I open it up and am shocked at what I'm reading.

> Cash: Rylee, I wanted to come over and go through some things of Jace's photos, etc. Can you let me know when I can do this. I have a key so I can come around when you're not in, if easier?

I scoff. Yeah, it would be easier. After the way he acted toward me over the last couple of weeks and toward me in general, I don't want to see him. I get he's feeling pain like nothing else too, but he has been so unfair toward me over the last six years, he can fucking wait. He was nice the day we had to say our goodbyes to Jace, but that doesn't make up for all the years he was shitty toward me for no reason. Anyway, the last thing I need right now is to see Cash, it's like a kick in the gut. He isn't the image of Jace, but you can see the resemblance. However, it's the eyes. Jace definitely took his dad's eyes, and that is not something I can deal with. I don't text Cash back, instead I wrap myself up further in the covers and continue to chase Jace's smell and pray he will come and see me. The continued exhaustion takes me under.

Chapter 23

I stare past myself in the mirror. Just staring. I have never felt so drained in all my life. All I have done is sleep the last eight days. I feel like I have gone ten rounds with Mike Tyson, and I look it too, to be honest. My whole face is swollen, I can barely open my eyes from all the crying, I have huge lumps on my eyelids, and my skin is breaking out like a hormonal teenager's. How I have black circles under my eyes I will never know, I have slept my life away the last week. I haven't cared about myself or my appearance. I think I have showered maybe three times, if I remember right. I showered today, but I was ready to crawl back into bed as soon as I stepped out.

The effort of sitting at the dressing table and getting ready has taken every ounce of strength I have. It was Bridget ringing me that made me get up. She told me the car will pick me up at 11:00 a.m. Today is the day we say our final goodbye to Jace. I kept thinking as the days went on, I would accept it more, but I don't. I don't think I ever will.

I have had so much time to think this week, I can't help but ask why. Why did he take the Xanax and Valium, why did he get in that car, but I know I will never get those answers, because the only person that can tell us that is no longer here. I have put myself in a state this week trying to wrap my head around it, trying to think of the weeks leading up to what happened if I noticed him being extra tired or if he was stressed. Work stressed Jace but the same amount it would stress anyone with a large workload. It's not Jace, and this is what I'm struggling to accept. I'm not saying he wouldn't take Xanax or Valium, but he wouldn't hide it or not tell me, or at least Cash. I just can't get my head around it. I know this is playing on Cash's mind too, but we have to let it go, we have no choice but to.

My phone chimes, signaling I have a text message.

Toni: I love you, see you soon

As much as I'm dreading seeing everyone, I can't wait for a hug from her and to see her, smell her. Jace always felt like home, but Toni is like the home away from home for me. I can be myself around her and act how I want, and she would never think any less of me and vice versa. She knows when I need to laugh, cry, and scream without me even saying anything, so I know today she will be my rock.

I continue getting ready, I don't care what I look like, but I owe it to Jace to at least try. I pile the concealer under my eyes, trying to cover the black circles, and dab away at the tops of my eyes, but it does nothing for me. My eyes are so swollen. I apply a tiny bit of waterproof mascara and that's it.

Bridget text me during the week, telling me, if I was okay with it, we were going to not wear black. Jace was full of sunshine and happiness, and we want his day to reflect that. I look on the bed at the royal-blue dress I picked out today. As soon as I saw it, it reminded me of his eyes. That unique blue I will never see again. The dress is a plain, midi-style with three-quarter length sleeves. I actually remember buying it, and the only reason I did was because it reminded me of his eyes. I have never worn it, I just left it in the closet. I pull my hair back in a ponytail, not bothering to style it. My body is shutting down on me already. I slip myself into the dress and look in the mirror. I stare at the blank space behind me.

Whenever I used to check my outfit or makeup and hair in the mirror, Jace would be lying on the bed because I always took so long to get ready, he would always be waiting for me. He would be on his phone most of the time, but sometimes I would catch him staring at me. Sometimes full of heat, but sometimes full of pure love. He watched me like I was the meaning to life.

I stare at the empty spot on the bed, his side of the bed which is still untouched, and close my eyes in the hopes that when I open them, he will be there staring back at me with that love. I wish this was a nightmare I could wake up from. It's never going to be, though.

I glance at the bedside clock, realizing I have five minutes before they will be here, I grab my bag and a coat, heading straight out the door before I can think anymore. If I do, I'll talk myself out of going. I walk outside, the fresh air helping me breathe a little easier. I stand there, looking up at the sky. Listening to the silence. Luckily, our apartment is backed away from the busy roads, so it's nice and quiet.

I listen to the birds tweeting away, giving a false sense of reality that it's a happy moment. Birds always sound so happy, but this moment is anything but. I stare up at the blue sky and the beaming sunshine. Weirdly enough, in Baltimore in February, it's usually icy and gray skies, but the sun is out in full force today. Jace was everyone's light in their life, his day could be nothing but bright.

I glance up to the road ahead and see the black car in the distance. It slowly crawls toward me. As it pulls up, I let out a breath, not realizing I was holding it in. Boh gets out of the car, walking up to me and pulling me in for a tight hug. I sink into Boh's hold for a minute.

"Come on, let's get in the car, Rylee."

I walk to the car, holding on to Boh for dear life, like he is my lifeline. I don't want to start everyone off crying, so I try to hold my tears at bay as best as I can as I take a seat inside the car. It's an open back car, so I take a seat next to Bridget, who is in a beautiful purple knee-length dress. She leans over, giving me a kiss on my cheek, no doubt feeling the wetness there. I smile at her as she grasps my hand in a tight grip, holding on and not letting go. We all need each other today, and I'm so lucky I have them here beside me. Cash and Boh are sitting next to each other, in their dark-gray suits with a navy-blue shirt underneath. I smile at Boh who returns the sad smile, and I look over at Cash, waiting to see his reaction.

I haven't spoken to him since the hospital. I didn't text him back that day, but Boh came to the apartment the day after with Cash's key. He text me before to tell me he would be popping in. He knocked on my bedroom door and popped his head in. I think he could tell I wasn't ready to talk, so he left me alone pretty quickly. I believe they were wanting photos for the funeral, but I didn't ask too many questions because the last thing I was thinking about was what photos need to be selected. I know it needed to be done, but it wasn't something my brain had the capacity to deal with. He peers over, like he is trying to find something. What, I don't know. I continue to stare at him and let him roam my face, then he nods his head toward me and looks out the window. I sigh and lean back in my seat. I guess we are back to this. I at least thought we would be a united front for today, but I guess not.

When we get close to the church, I'm taken aback by how many people are here, there is a line wrapped around the building. I'm not shocked, Jace was loved more than I have ever known anyone to be loved before, I just didn't think they would all turn up. And not speaking with anyone this week, I wasn't sure who would come. I turn to each person in the car, they all have their heads down like it pains them to see how loved Jace was. It's just another reminder of what we have all lost.

The car pulls up outside the entrance to the church, people are stood to the side so we can have room to get out and look at the flowers that are placed outside the church. I step out of the car, bringing my hand to my mouth and have to hold my sob in when I see the flowers.

"The Hammer," I choke out, Thor's hammer. The gray flowers perfectly detail the shape of Thor's hammer, the color, everything. It's perfect. I have never seen anything like it. I smile.

Jace would love this so much, he would be obsessing over it. I then laugh a little because if he could hear me calling this a hammer, he would give me the biggest lecture and tell me to stop winding him up. I can't believe they got this. I look over all the other flowers, I see son and nephew, then what I see next has me breaking out into an immediate sob. I clutch my stomach, wishing for the sick feeling to go. I stare at a big red heart in the middle with the initials J & R in blue flowers in the middle. It's so beautiful. Boh grabs me from behind, holding me close to his chest. I try to stop my sobbing, but it just continues.

As we walk into the church, I stop at the entrance, gasping for air as I see the coffin at the back on a stand, my heart beating too fast for me to catch my breath. I close my eyes, silence falls upon me but also the faint sounds of the birds tweeting away from outside, and the sobbing noises from Bridget. I pinch my thumb to ground me. I can hear, I can feel. A hand touches my shoulder and everything around me comes back to life. I slowly open my eyes, blinking rapidly, trying to keep the tears at bay.

There is a big picture of Jace at the front. This was at one of the birthdays, and it's one of our favorite pictures of Jace because he was midconversation with me as Bridget called his name, then he turned and looked straight at the camera, with his normal smile on his face and a beer in his hand.

Jace had a will, according to a text Bridget sent me, and he wanted to be cremated. The thought killed me, knowing he won't be whole anymore, but I have to keep reminding myself he will always live whole in my heart. We haven't spoken about the ashes, but I trust whatever Cash and the family chose was the right decision. Once we have taken our seats, they let everyone else in, when I turn around, I see familiar faces, some giving me a sad smile, some already crying. This is easily their biggest room, and the seats are filling up fast. Once everyone is in, there are people standing at the back, and it makes me smile inside. I hope he knew how loved he was.

The funeral officiant speaks, but I don't comprehend a thing as I stare at the remembrance card in my hand. There's a picture of Jace and I on the back, me smiling at the camera and him looking down at me like I was his everything. The picture is beautiful, and I have never seen it before. *I need this framed.* I will never again smile like that.

"Rylee." Bridget nudges me. I glance at her and then up to the funeral officiant, I haven't heard one thing he said.

"You don't have to do this," she whispers, grasping my hands. I then realize it's time for me to go up and say some words. Bridget had text me during the week, asking if I wanted to, and I did, I still do, but I didn't plan any words like I wanted to, I couldn't. I thought it would get easier, but every time I tried, I would just cry. I smile at Bridget. "It's okay." I stand up, walking to the front. I look over at the box and then at everyone else. I take a deep breath, thinking how much I want to do him proud.

"I just wanted to firstly say it shows how much Jace was loved by seeing every single one of you. There are hundreds here, this shows how much of a special person he was." Many people are smiling and nodding their heads.

"As you all know, Jace and I were together for six years." I swallow the lump already forming. "I still remember the morning after meeting him and waking up in his bed, in his shirt." It's then I spot Toni smiling at me. I know she has great memories of Jace as well as me. They were partners in crime against me sometimes. They had a special bond, so I know this has hit her too. "He was so casual like I belonged there, like I had been in his bed and in his shirt every morning." I smile to myself, thinking back to that morning at how mortified I was after what he had told me.

"I know he knew as much as I did that from that moment, I was his as much as he was mine. He told me when he dropped me home that morning that he would be seeing me again. I then realized only weeks later how utterly in love I was with him. How could you not?" For a split second, the conversation I had with Cash about Jace's mom pops into my head. She really did miss out on such a special person.

"Jace was the light in everyone's life. If anyone needed cheering up, just one look at Jace would make you smile." I smile to myself and see everyone smiling, some crying while also nodding, agreeing with me. I turn, glimpsing the box he's concealed in. "You promised me always, Jace, but you couldn't give me forever. I can't bring myself to say goodbye to you because I know the minute I do, this goodbye will mean forever, and this wasn't the type of forever I had in my head for us. So, this isn't goodbye, this is just goodbye for now. See you in my dreams. I love you. Always." I look down as the tears pour out of my eyes. "Forever," I whisper.

Boh comes up and wraps his arms around me while I cry into his chest and walks me back to our seats. I sit there like that, crying the rest of the funeral. I wish I could have paid attention to the whole thing, but in all honesty, this isn't something I ever imagined having or would want to remember. I said my goodbye to Jace back at the hospital, I didn't want to have to do this again.

Chapter 24

The rest of the funeral is a blur, I cried and cried until the end, and Boh held me the entire time. We are now on our way to the bar that Cash hired out for the evening so everyone could celebrate Jace's life together. Boh is sporting a brave face today, but I know he's dying inside. He has always been tight lipped on emotions, he is the joker of the family, but I know he hides a lot behind the laughs and jokes. I wish he wouldn't, but it's the way he has always been since I have known him.

Cash has been staring out the window the entire time. I don't want to go to the bar, I want to go home and get into bed and hope I can smell Jace. It will be like he never left, but Bridget has asked I try for at least an hour.

Toni also approached me at the end of the funeral, when everyone was coming over and passing on their condolences, and asked me to come. She didn't say it to make me feel bad but reminded me that Jace would have wanted me and everyone else to celebrate his life, and she is right.

There were so many people that Boh had to say at the funeral that unfortunately not everyone could come to the wake as we couldn't fit everyone. People thankfully understood. I appreciate them, but I blanked people out when the funeral ended and just kept saying my thank-yous and letting the next person approach me. I felt numb toward the end and now I'm drained. I'm here because I need to be, not because I want to be. I want to be at home, on my own, not surrounded by people either crying, laughing, or being drunk and crying. I can't think of anything worse.

I sit at a table on my own, watching everyone around me but not paying attention to everything they are doing. To people, I will appear fine, and that is what I want. I don't want them hovering around me, thinking they need to be with me or keep asking if I'm okay. Of course I'm not okay, it's a stupid question to ask people when they have just lost someone, but we all do it, because what else do you say? Toni comes up to me with a drink in her hand and pushes it into my face.

"Drink."

"I didn't really want to drink tonight, Ton." I wince.

"There is no way you are doing this afternoon and evening without drinking, you will need it with every other person coming up to you asking if you're okay when you clearly are not."

She is right, I probably will need it, the drink will make it easier. I don't want to drink too much though because I know it will go the other way and I will just cry uncontrollably.

"True," I say, taking a sip. The sharp burn in my throat and the fire pit in my stomach cause my lip to curl up.

"What the fuck is this?"

"Vodka tonic, but I added in a dash of tequila for the extra burn." She smiles innocently at me.

"You're a masochist, you know that," I snarl at her.

"I know, baby." She puckers her lips at me. I appreciate Toni being the way she is. She isn't moping, I know deep down today is killing her as well, but she is trying to be as normal as possible in the hopes it will help me.

I keep the drink away from my lips. After that, I'm sure she's just trying to get me black-out drunk so I don't remember anything going on in my life. Although, the more I think about that, the more appealing it becomes.

"Ergh" comes from behind me. Before I can ask her what is wrong, James walks toward us, like he has the weight of the world on his shoulders. I recognize the look well.

"Hey," he mumbles. His eyes are bloodshot, which is the obvious tell he has been crying a lot. He bends down to give me a kiss on the cheek. He has also been drinking a lot, by the smell of it. I don't blame him, that is how some people get through grief. It's meant to make them forget but does it really? Or does it make them think more and think back to every little argument, every little hiccup in their relationship with that person that then drives you into a deeper hole. I can imagine this is what it would do to me, which has me putting my drink on the table and telling myself I will not be drinking anything else tonight.

Although, Jace and I rarely argued and never had any major issues, but even just remembering a night I went to bed without telling him I loved him will send me into a bigger downward spiral than I'm already in.

James takes a seat next to me, he doesn't acknowledge Toni. I think he knows by now she is not his biggest fan, and he is probably not even caring about pleasing people. He just huffs and looks down. The words *How you doing*? go to slip off my tongue but then I remember how much it annoys me when people ask me this question, so instead I place my hand on his knee and give him a squeeze. He glances up at me, giving me a look that says a thousand words. Even though him and Jace had drifted, they were still friends, and he will have thousands of fond memories with Jace.

"He would have been proud of you today," James whispers so quietly only I would catch on to what he said due to the closeness.

A lump forms in my throat. "Thanks." I don't know what else he wants me to say.

We sit there in what would normally be an awkward silence, but it feels nice to sit in stillness and be here with someone who truly knew Jace. I look up, and straight in front of me across the room is Cash staring at me and then he glares down. I follow his line of sight and see he is staring at my hand on James's leg. His nostrils flare and then he clenches his fists. I pull my hand back from James's leg as if it burned me. James looks up at me and frowns, as if to ask what happened. I offer him a small smile and glance back up, but Cash is nowhere in sight. I don't know why he was glaring at me like that, and I don't know why I pulled my hand away as if I was doing something wrong. It was an automatic reaction, but I was just helping James. We all need someone to be there, not necessarily saying anything but them being by your side helps more than anyone would ever know.

"I can't stop thinking about him, Ry. I see him in my dreams." I swing my gaze to James.

"He came to see you too?" I ask eagerly. James's eyebrows are furrowed.

"What do you mean, came to see me?"

"You said you see him in your dreams?" I don't want to outright say Jace visited me, but I wanted to know what James means by seeing his face.

"I just mean I keep seeing his huge smile. The—" He sighs and looks down, playing with his hands. "The night of the accident, at the bar, he was so happy." A tear drops from his eye. "He couldn't wait to get home to tell you about the vacation, he was showing everyone the pictures and—"

"What are you talking about, what vacation?" *I don't know anything about a vacation. What is he talking about?*

James turns ghostly white. "I-I—" He takes a deep breath, then stares into my eyes.

"Ry, I'm so sorry, I thought you knew," he says, leaving me gutted to the core. Jace booked us a vacation and he never made it home to tell me. I need to find Bridget. She would have known about this.

I stand up, ready to find Bridget, and feel a touch on my hand. I look down at James, and he has no tears left and appears blank, like there is no one there, like he has put a mask on.

"I'm sorry," he says before standing up and walking away. My eyebrows scrunch as he walks away but then I look around the room for Bridget. I walk past people, frantically asking if anyone has seen her. Someone points over to the corner of the bar, and she's talking to one of Jace's cousins. I rush over to her, wanting to know what James was talking about. I don't even give her a chance to say anything or even wait until she has finished talking.

"Did Jace book us a vacation?" I say as soon as I approach her.

She looks at me wide-eyed and doesn't say anything, but her reaction says everything I need to know.

"Why didn't you tell me?" I choke out, trying not to let the tears fall.

"It wouldn't have done you any good knowing, Rylee."

"I want to know, though. Where was it? When?" I want to know everything, now that I know, it's going to kill me either way. Jace's cousin excuses himself while Bridget pats the chair next to her. I sit, not taking my eyes off her.

"Remember at Cash's birthday dinner I mentioned Tulum?" I nod at her. "He had booked a beautiful beach house for you as a surprise, he was going to tell you the day before your birthday, and you were flying out on your birthday," she says, tears welling in her eyes.

I stare at the table. *That's in six months, he had it all planned out?* The sick feeling in my stomach that hasn't left since the day I realized it was Jace lying in that bed, gets stronger.

"He—" She wipes the tears away from her eyes, grabbing my hands in both of hers, stroking them. She wipes the never-ending trail of tears trickling down my face.

"He called me the day of the accident, telling me he had booked and paid for it all. He was so happy and couldn't wait to tell you, Rylee," Bridget cries out.

"No. I can't do this," I say, standing abruptly. "I need to go." I walk away from Bridget, from everyone. Someone behind me is calling my name, but I couldn't tell you who it is. I feel like I'm underwater. I run past everyone in a blur, not even taking in who I'm pushing out of the way. I feel like if I don't get out of here soon, a wave will take me under, and this time, I won't come up for air, I'll drown.

Chapter 25

I don't remember getting home last night; all I remember is getting out of the Uber and walking up to the entrance doors to the apartment building. I don't even remember booking the Uber. After hearing Jace had booked the vacation for us, the day he had the accident, the one we were so excited for and he deserved more than anything, it pushed me back into the black hole I thought I was escaping from.

I don't think I will ever escape. Every time a memory is brought up, every time I think about his unforgettable face, every time I think about his tender touch, the way his face would light up when he walked through our apartment doors and he saw my face after a long day. I'll always be treading the edges, just waiting to fall. Heartbreak and grief together are like a hole so deep you can't climb out of it, but, at the same time, it's like someone dropping a ladder into that hole for you to grab onto to make your way back up to the light but not wanting to. I don't deserve to be brought back to the light. If Jace can't be there with me, then why should I? I don't want to leave this darkness. Jace was my light, and without him, there's no light left in my life.

I curl further into my covers, that wave of grief washing over me again. I know I need to get up and shower, but I can't, my body physically won't let me. I pick up my phone, opening my browser to what I was looking at last night before finally drifting off to sleep. The tears threaten to bleed from my eyes again, that's what it feels like now, it feels like my eyes are bleeding because they are so sore from all the crying.

When I got home, I logged into Jace's emails, as we always had each other's passwords for personal email accounts just in case we ever needed it. I found the confirmation and looked up where he had booked. It is simply stunning. He had booked us two weeks in a private beach house sitting on Paradise Beach in Tulum. The beach house is surrounded by palm trees and the sand is a dusty shade of white. I can only imagine how soft that would feel under my feet. The ocean, only meters from the entrance of the beach house, is the perfect shade of blue, just like Jace's eyes. Thinking back to last night when it hit me that Jace and I would never walk across this sand, we would never experience this beautiful place together, makes me feel sick all over again. He picked the most perfect place for me, for us, and we will never stand there together, we will never have vacations together again. I sob into my pillow again and again, letting my already-broken heart bleed out.

Minutes, hours later, who knows, my intercom buzzes, and I let it keep buzzing. Talking, let alone seeing someone, is nowhere near the top of my list. The buzzing stops and I sink further in my bed.

A door clicks. For God's sake. Only three people now have keys to this apartment. Toni, Bridge, and Cash.

"Rylee . . ." Bridget's gentle voice floats through the apartment. I sink even further into my bed, praying she will not come in here and will think I'm out. Of course that does not happen, and my bedroom door opens.

"Rylee," she whispers.

If I pretend I'm asleep, she may just leave. I don't answer or open my eyes and stay as still as I can, even trying to even out my breathing. The bed dips beside me and her hand starts stroking my hair. My emotions are all over the place. As much as I don't want to see or speak to anyone, her touch is like something I have longed for. Losing someone you loved more than anything, and the heartbreak that comes along with that grief, is something that not just mentally hurts, it physically hurts, and I always found, growing up, no matter how much something hurt me the comfort from my mom always helped even if it was just a little bit. Having Bridge stroking my hair right now brings back the memories of my mom doing this exact thing, and in a weird way, with my eyes closed, I can pretend it is my mom. Of course, reality rears its nasty head because my mom always had her own smell, and though Bridget's smell is lovely, it's not my mom and it's not Jace. A sob I didn't even feel rising escapes my mouth before I can stop it.

"Oh, Rylee," Bridge whimpers out.

She lies next to me, wrapping her arms tightly around me and hugs me.

"I looked at the place he booked, Bridge," I choke out.

"It's stunning, isn't it?"

I nod into her chest. "He did good."

"When will this get better for us, Bridge, when will it stop hurting, when will it stop burning. I feel like I'm surrounded by fire, just waiting for someone to come put it out, but no one comes, Bridge. No one will ever be able to put this fire out, no one will be able to stop the burning."

"I don't think it ever will, Ry. I think the burning is something we will have to learn to live with." She sighs.

We lie there in silence for a while.

"I need to text Cash," Bridge says after a while. "I told him I would let him know how you are."

I sit up, looking at Bridge, confused. "Why would Cash care how I am?" Bridge always knew how I felt about Cash, how I wasn't his biggest fan and vice versa, even though the family always told me that's just how Cash is. *"He's not a people person."*

"You're family, Ry. Of course he cares." She frowns at me.

I shrug and slip out of bed, going to my en suite bathroom. I have been needing to pee for a while now but holding it in because I couldn't bring myself to move. I go back into my bedroom, and Bridge is no where to be seen, so I head out to the kitchen. She is emptying my dishwasher and wiping down the counters as she goes along. I walk to the fridge, grabbing a bottle of water, and start walking back to my bed.

"Rylee."

I turn around, looking at her a long, and low sigh leaves her lips as her shoulders sag. Her vacant, puffy eyes meet mine.

"You can't spend all your time in bed. I know how you are hurting, Ry. The pain isn't skin deep, it's bone deep. I know," she says, holding her chest, tears welling in her eyes. "But Jace wouldn't want you like this. He wouldn't want any of us like this."

I nod, knowing she is right. I have tried telling myself this over and over again, but the feeling won't go away. I'm so weak, everything just hurts.

"I spoke to Toni earlier," she states. She turns around, continuing to empty the dishwasher.

"She is coming around tonight. She is going to stay the night and you are going to have a girls' night, Ry. You need it."

"Okay," I mutter. I walk back to bed. I will get up once Ton is here. For now, I'm going to sleep because that is all my body is screaming out for.

Chapter 26

Toni left early morning as she needed to go to work, she said she would play hooky, but I basically forced her to get ready and leave. She kept saying she would stay another night, and I could tell she actually wanted to, but I think, in a weird way, I need to get used to being on my own and not lying in bed all day. She brought bags of chocolate and wine. We binge watched *Spinning Out* on Netflix, and I loved it. We only paused if we needed to go the toilet or top our wine up. It was the first night I have felt normal, and, as bad as it sounds, Jace wasn't mentioned once. I did, for a few hours, forget every shitty thing going on in my life and enjoyed time with my friend.

I need to start facing facts: Jace isn't here, and he isn't coming back. As much as even thinking it pains me, it's been only nine days, and I swear I still feel his touch and smell him in certain rooms I walk in. Especially his office. I have only been in there twice, and I can't bring myself to go in there often. There is too much of him in there, everything he loved, his whole life is in that room, so for now, I keep it shut.

I texted Rachel this morning, telling her I am coming back to work next week. She has been texting and ringing nonstop. I told her I would reach out when I was ready. She still sent me daily texts, telling me she was thinking of me and will always be there. She was at the funeral, but I didn't get to speak to her as much as I would have liked to.

Rachel thinks I should take more time off, but I can't sit in this apartment day in and day out again. I got like this when my mom died, staying in bed all day, crying, not wanting to talk to anyone. I'm slowly going back to that again, actually, I am already there, but back then, I had Jace to pull me out of it. Don't get me wrong, I have Jace's family and all my friends but it's not the same. I have to pull myself out of it this time, I'm the only one who can do it.

My phone chimes for the one-hundredth time this week. I pick it up, seeing a notification I have many unread messages. I need to eventually go through and reply to people, but now is not the time.

The last message is from Cash. I open it up.

> Cash: Rylee. Can I pop around today? I need to go through some of Jace's documents he has in the office.

Of course Cash is back to work, like father, like son. I'm sure there is loads of stuff in the office that Cash needs, Jace used to work from home a lot, so he had a lot of confidential information in the safe and many, many files. It will probably take Cash a while to go through it all. As much as I don't want to be here when he does it, I really cannot be bothered to go out today. Yes,

I am trying to make myself better but baby steps. I sigh, replying and telling him that's fine and to come over whenever.

I don't get a reply from Cash but a couple of hours later, the door buzzes. Assuming it's Cash, I buzz him up without checking. I open my front door and head back into the living room and turn the TV back on. I have started rewatching *Twilight*. This is my comfort show, without a doubt. I have lost count of how many times I have seen this film.

A throat clears behind me. I'm surprised Cash has actually came to say hello. I turn around and am taken aback to see James standing there.

I jump up. "James? I didn't know you were coming over today?"

He rubs the back of his neck and shifts from foot to foot.

"Yeah. I thought you might not want to see me if I just texted, so I thought I would just drop in. I was quite surprised to see you just buzzed me in, were you expecting someone else?" He eyes me up with raised eyebrows.

"Yeah, uh, Cash." James stills, titling his head to the side, squinting at me before dropping his chin to the floor. "He said he was popping over today to go through some work stuff in Jace's office," I clarify, pointing to the door—not that I need to.

James glances up, nodding slowly, then continues to shift and fidget.

"Would you like a coffee or—"

"A coffee would be great."

I don't want to sit and have a small talk with James, but I feel rude standing here not offering.

I walk past him, making my way to the kitchen. He follows me in, taking a seat at one of the island stalls.

"I actually came over here to say sorry for the other night at Jace's wake, Ry." He sighs, looking down at his fingers on the kitchen counter in front of him, playing with the skin around his nails. Before I can tell him to not worry about it and that he has nothing to be sorry for, he continues. "I shouldn't have mentioned the vacation, it wasn't my place. I just assumed you knew." He looks at me, pleading, clearly thinking I'm annoyed with him.

I shake my head lightly, walking over to him. I grab his hands and hold them, stopping him from picking the skin around his nails.

"James, it's fine. Honest. I didn't know, but I'm glad you mentioned it. Although it did send me into a bit of a dark hole and I was in a bad way, I'm glad I know now." I smile at him. "I logged onto Jace's emails and found the booking. It's beautiful and just another reminder of how much he loved me. Although that hurts, at the same time, it fills me with love." I shrug slightly. "It's hard to explain."

He nods at me, glancing at our hands, and as I go to pull them away, he grips them and holds them. "You know I will always be here for you, Rylee," he says, staring into my eyes. I smile politely. I know his way of being a friend, but it feels weird.

"I know."

"Rylee . . ." There's venom in a voice to the side of me. Cash is standing there staring at me, then at James, then he looks down at our joint hands. *Fuck.*

"Cash," I say, pulling my hands away from James's. It was totally innocent, but I remember the way Cash glared at us when I had my hand on his knee at the wake. Now this. Even I can admit it doesn't look great. Adding to the list, Cash, for some reason, despises James. *This isn't good.*

James scoots his chair back and stands up, glancing at Cash and then at me, eyes wide as if he got caught doing something he shouldn't have.

"I, uh, best, erm, go." He points behind him at the front door. "Rain check on the coffee?" he says.

"Yeah, okay." The way James is acting, isn't helping matters. I don't tell him we will rearrange. That will just add fuel to the fire for Cash, and I cannot deal with the moody asshole right now.

James walks out, having to bypass Cash. His jaw clenched and nostrils flared. James picks up his pace and, to be honest, I can't blame him. Cash has always had this aura about him, letting you know he has another side to him you don't want to unleash.

The apartment door closes, and Cash turns his anger toward me. "What was he doing here?" he spits.

My eyebrows raise at the fucking audacity he has to question who I have in my apartment.

"Excuse me?"

"You heard me!"

"Firstly"—I point to the floor—"this is *my* apartment. I will have whoever I want in here. And secondly, don't you dare question me as if I'm guilty of something."

Cash raises his eyebrow as if to say, *Well, are you?* and I let out a slight chuckle.

"Fuck off, Cash. Seriously." I don't have to pussyfoot around him now. Jace isn't here. I always respected him for Jace and put up with his shit. Not anymore. I thought at the hospital he may have turned a new leaf but clearly not. If anyone wanted to know what Jekyll and Hyde acted like, he's standing right in front of me.

His nostrils flare like he wants to tell me exactly what is on his mind. He stares me down, but I don't look away. He has another thing coming if he thinks I'm backing down from him.

"Go grab whatever it is you needed and get the fuck out of my apartment, Cash." I grab my bottle of water off the kitchen counter, brushing past him as I walk back into the living room and pressing playing from where I was before James turned up.

Cash doesn't say a word, he enters Jace's office and slams the door behind him. Tears well in my eyes once again. This time, it doesn't feel like grief, it's anger. Anger that I have to deal with such a prick. I hope once he gets what he needs, he fucks off, and doesn't come back. I would be happy never seeing Cash Stiles again, that's for sure.

Chapter 27

I'm making myself chicken stir fry, still raging from earlier. *How dare he!* The more time goes on, the angrier I get. I fell asleep while watching *Twilight*. When I woke up hours later, there was a blanket over me with the TV turned off and a fresh bottle of water sitting on the table. The fucking audacity. He wants to come into my apartment, accuse me of God knows what, speak down to me like I'm his fucking child, and then covers me with a blanket while I sleep. If this is his way of apologizing, he needs a reality check. I'm seething, and the annoying thing is, I would never normally get this annoyed over something so small. I'm blaming it on my emotions being all over the place.

I finish cooking my stir fry and sit down at the island, playing around with the food, not feeling all that hungry. I have eaten little over the last two weeks, and I can feel it in my clothes. Not that I'm complaining, but I normally have a great appetite, and as of late, it's nonexistent. I sigh, placing down my fork. I know what I need. A good drink, it's been a while and there is one person always down to drink, without question. I jump up off the stool, heading to the living room to grab my phone. I bring up Toni's number, and she picks up on the second ring. This girl never leaves me hanging.

"What are you doing?" I say without even saying hello.

"Sitting in my pj's perving over Vin Diesel in *Pitch Black*. Want to join?" she says with hope in her voice.

"I'll join you, but I need alcohol involved."

"Now you're talking, but I'll do you one better. We get ready and go out drinking, not indoors."

I groan because I knew she would try this, but I don't want to be around people, especially if I bump into someone I know. They will ask me the obvious question, and I don't need that when I'm drunk. I just want a night of forgetting. I don't want to remember anything; I want one normal night with my girl.

"Do we have to? I just want a night to forget, Ton."

"I know you do, but sitting in drinking is not going to do that, Ry. Going out, music, dancing, shots. That will make you forget, I'll help you forget. Trust me?"

"Okay." I sigh. I will always trust this girl with my life, and if she says she will make me forget, she will.

Toni squeals down the phone, nearly bursting an eardrum, rattling off that she is chucking on a tracksuit and heading over. I hang up the phone feeling somewhat lighter, I know this night out is just what I need, and I couldn't think of anyone better to spend it with.

After spending three hours, yes, three fucking hours, getting ready, we finally arrive at Lockdown. This is one of the best clubs in Baltimore, it's also huge, so the chances of bumping into someone I know are slim. Toni is dressed in a strappy tight and very short silver sequin dress with her ash blonde hair cascading down her back in light soft curls. She looks like an absolute vision, and every guy she is walking past is literally wiping the drool away. She spent probably two of the three hours getting ready on our makeup alone. She has given us smokey eyes and has gone very heavy on the makeup. I love makeup but I'm useless at it. Whenever we go out, she always gives me a huge confidence boost with how she does my makeup.

She picked out a dress for me, telling me I needed to go with a mini dress like hers. I always settle for a midi dress as I love when they hit the knees and somewhat hide my chunky thighs, but Toni was not having it tonight. I am in spaghetti-strap bright-red dress with a cutout back. I felt a bit shameful when I checked myself in the mirror.

From the outside, it would look like we're two girls out on the prowl tonight, but that is far from the truth. I couldn't imagine touching another man like that again! I just want a normal night tonight and to feel happy with myself. If dressing up is what it takes, then I'll take it. I need a lift me up and this is it.

Toni and I are at the bar, waiting for our drinks, it was too loud to even hear what she ordered us, but I'm past the stage of caring. I just want to get drunk. Men keep approaching us, and from what I can tell, and slightly hear now and then, Toni has gone with us being lesbians and here with each other. She grabs my hand every time, apologizing to them. We used to always do this when we were younger and were being hit on by a guy we did not want to talk to.

Toni is single and can do what she wants, but this is why she is the best friend a girl could ask for; she turns down guys I know are her type just so we can have our night together. I know I don't deserve this girl; she puts everything into our friendship, and I put all but half. I know she understands I'm just always running around doing stuff, but it doesn't make me feel any less guilty. We grab our drinks and head straight to the dance floor, doing what we came here to do: get drunk and dance.

The night passes by in a blur, and I have no idea what I am drinking now, but what I do know is I feel great. I feel better than great. I feel amazing. Ton and I have not stopped dancing, my feet hurt but I welcome the ache. I don't want this night to end.

Toni moves closer, shouting in my ear, "Shall we go?"

I lean back away from her and shrug.

"This music is not it," she says.

She is right, it changed about an hour ago. Toni and I have no idea what music this is now. I'm thinking the latest chart music, which we clearly don't know anything about, then I feel old as the thought passes through my head. I nod at her as we sway toward the doors, still moving our hips even though we don't know the songs.

As we squeeze our way outside, the cold air hits our face. We let out a giggle. I was already feeling drunk but now I'm feeling *drunnnkkk*. We hold on to each other while walking away from the club. We are giggling at nothing. My ankles keep buckling as I walk. My feet are killing me, but the drunkenness makes the pain bearable. I can only imagine the state we look right now, but I'm too drunk to even care. I have no idea how long we have been walking, but we stop looking at each other, look around and then burst out laughing again.

"Where are we even going?" I laugh out. Toni is bent over, laughing, the kind of laugh that has tears leaking from your eyes.

"I have no idea," she says, still laughing and holding her stomach.

"Come on, I think the cab office is down here." I loaded up my Uber app back at the club, but it said there weren't any available. We walk down a street which seems lively, there are loads of pubs and clubs lined up. People drunk-shouting, some sitting in the corners of the shut shop doorways eating greasy food, looking like the best thing ever presented to them on this earth. The smells make my stomach moan.

"Ahh, I need food," I say, eyeing up people's food as we walk past.

"McDs?" Toni smirks.

"Yes!" I shout way too enthusiastically, gathering the attention of some near passerbys.

Toni stops, bends down, unstraps her heels, and takes them off, holding my arm as she does. While I wait, I look around and that's when I see it. Freedom. Where we were the night Jace entered my life. I stand rooted to the spot, staring at the club. Everyone around me becomes distant, and I barely hear anything else. I stare at the huge red sign on the front of the building.

"Rylee. Rylee. Look at me, babe." Toni is snapping her fingers in my face. I break out of my stare and all the noise around us comes back full force. Toni's brows are drawn together as her wide, panicked eyes flit between mine. She realized what I was staring at.

"I want to go in," I whisper. It's probably the drink telling me this. I think if I was sober, I would have run a mile away by now, but it's like a magnet is pulling me toward it.

Toni is shaking her head. "No, you don't, Ry."

"Please." I beg her with my eyes. "Please." I squeeze her hand.

She takes a deep breath and grabs my hand. "C'mon, then," she huffs. "I promised you I would make you forget tonight, Ry."

I pull on her arm, stopping her. "You have. I have had the best night!" I don't want her thinking all her effort was for nothing, I don't remember the last time I laughed so much. She nods, looking down.

It was the best until now, but that's not her fault.

We get to the doors, and the bouncers stand aside, letting us straight in, not even asking to check our ID. Toni takes one look at me, as if asking if I'm sure I want to do this. I give her a sharp nod and we walk in.

Freedom was always one big open club, it's huge in here with extremely high ceilings. I look around and nothing has changed. *Not a thing.* The DJ stand is still where it always was, the bar is exactly the same. The black and silver stripe walls haven't changed. I just stand there, taking everything in. The music is pumping through the speakers, everyone is happy and dancing away to much better music than what was playing in Lockdown. I walk up the stairs toward the long bar at the very back, and there is a bartender ready to take my order. I order Toni and me a vodka and cola. I probably shouldn't drink anymore alcohol, but I need it to take the edge off. Toni saddles up on one of the chairs beside me, waving down another bartender.

"I already ordered drinks."

"We need shots," she deadpans. She orders us two tequila shots from another bartender as our drinks are served. The guy makes quick work of pouring our shots and puts them in front of us with a slice of lemon sitting in the top and places the saltshaker between us. Toni grabs my hand and shakes salt on the back, we look at each other as Toni raises her shot glass.

"To memories."

"To memories," I mumble out. We go straight in for the salt and then down the tequila. I don't even bother with the lemon, chucking it back on the bar. I welcome the burn the tequila leaves in my chest.

"Nothing's changed," I say. "Yet so much has." I didn't think I would get emotional in here but, looking around, it's like a film playing back. Observing the dance floor, I see me, Toni, Tash, Jayleigh, and Rosa all dancing. Happy in the moment, happy in life. I look over toward the restrooms and my stomach sinks. It's like an out of body experience. I see Jace as he bumps into my shoulder. I see it all. I look to my right and see him next to me, looking at me. The blue eyes staring back at me. The huge smile that lights up any room he walks in. I see him.

A sob escapes me as I feel a pull on my shoulders, then he disappears.

"Noo," I cry out.

"Come on, we are going," Toni states, pulling me away from the bar.

"No! He was there, Toni. He was there," I shout, trying to wrench away. Toni is dragging me out of the club, and I swear I see Jace staring back at me from the bar, sad that I'm leaving him. I scream and swing my arms around.

"Rylee, *stop*!" Toni shouts, but I don't stop. I keep swinging and screaming. My arms are connecting with something or someone, but I don't care. Hands grab me and then arms wrap around me, stopping me from moving. I don't stop screaming, I don't stop crying. I don't want to open my eyes because I know I won't see him. He will be gone, and I can't face losing him again. I cry and cry, unable to stop. I don't know how much time I sit there crying with my eyes closed. I can hear hushed voices around me, not caring what they are saying. I want Jace, that's all I want. An arm hooks under my legs and another supports my back, picking me up from the floor.

"Shh, I got you" is whispered in my ear. I rest my face on the hard broad chest, getting lost in the smell. It's not Jace, as much as I wish I was dreaming and it was, it's not, but whoever it is, feels warm and safe. I cry into the person's chest, gripping onto them for dear life, hoping they won't let me fall.

"No, don't let me go. Please," I cry out as they go to lower me.

"I need to get us in the cab, let me just put you down." I'm not paying attention to who is speaking, but they place me down on something soft which I can assume is the back of the cab.

"Go to sleep, Ry," the person murmurs, I grip onto their arm, needing to feel some comfort.

"I'm going to see Jace," I whisper as I let sleep take me, hoping to see his beautiful face again.

Chapter 28

Three months later...

Does life get easier when you lose someone you love? I don't think it does. I think you get better at dealing with the pain, at hiding it. You get so used to saying "I'm fine" that you start to believe it yourself, but when those nights creep in when it's just you and your thoughts alone, that's when you realize nothing got easier and the pain never went away. The pain is still very much there, lingering, waiting to shatter every façade you have built around yourself. You learn to live with that missing piece to the puzzle. A puzzle is never a full picture without it.

That's what I feel like, without Jace, there is always something missing. I will be out walking and just stop on the street, thinking I have forgotten something. I will go all day trying to work out what I have forgotten or left at home. You come to realize you forgot nothing; you left nothing at home. Jace is that missing piece to the puzzle and is gone forever.

When people ask me how I'm doing, it's always "I'm fine" with a smile. "The days are getting easier," "Time is a healer," that's what it will always be, because how do you explain this feeling to someone? How do you explain this hollow emptiness you have in the pit of your stomach, day in and day out. You can't. No one knows what to say to you, and to be honest, I don't even know what to say to myself. So the generic answer is what I go with. You learn to smile again, you learn to laugh again, but when you lie in bed at night, you let the tears fall and start all over again the following day. I have learned to live like this, and I'm okay with it. Is it healthy? Probably not, but it's what I have. I have my odd days when I wake up and smile and thank life I got to meet Jace and have him in my life, even if it wasn't for as long as I wanted. I try to be grateful for just that, but it never lasts.

"Night, Rylee," I snap out of the trance I was in. Harley peeks his head through my office door.

"Night, Harley. Have a good night." I smile at him. The fake smile I have learned to plaster on my face.

After being off for six weeks, my work piled up big time. Everyone in the office did what they could, but there was a lot of work that only I could do, so I have been having to catch up with it since being back.

I must admit, wine has been my best friend most nights. Only one or two, but just something to calm my nerves and help me sleep. It numbs me too, which helps. I never go over two glasses, what happened three months ago when I went out with Toni has made me realize alcohol is not the answer. The night is a blur, but when I woke up and realized I was laying on a man's chest on my sofa, I freaked out more than I ever have in my life. I thought the worst, and I was in an even worse state when I looked up and saw those blue eyes staring back at me. I was clinging to Cash like he was my lifeline, and I don't remember how I even got there. When Cash explained I freaked out in the club where I met Jace for the first time and hit Toni multiple times to the point she had to ring him to come and get me, I was traumatized.

Cash didn't look angry like I expected him to. He looked sad, slightly uncomfortable, which who the hell could blame him? His dead son's girlfriend was hanging off him like a koala bear. When Cash said I begged him not to let go, he said he felt bad and that I was in a bad way. He was worried to leave me, apparently. I profusely apologized; he said it was fine. He left pretty quick after that, and I have spoken to him twice over text, and it's been to say "*Hi*" and "*hope you're okay*."

Bridge and Bohdi ring me every week, they won't forget me or leave me. I have people at work constantly checking in on me and saying if the work is getting too much, then I need to just say. But to be honest, it has helped me. I still think a lot but a little less now that work takes up most of my time. You could say I have turned into a workaholic. If I wake up in the night and can't get back to sleep, I reach for my laptop and work. I don't work from home anymore. That wasn't helping, so I always come into the office. As much as I hate having to plaster on a fake smile, I know if I stay at home, I will get myself so deep into a hole I won't be able to remove myself from it.

Bridge and Boh are coming for dinner tonight, and I'm so excited to see them. I was worried when we lost Jace I would lose them too, but they have treated me no different, if anything, I hear from them more than I ever have. I know they are doing the exact same as to what I am doing, pretending they are fine when deep down they are not. I can't wait to see them for selfish reasons. They know what I am going through. I don't have to pretend with them. I can share my grief with them, I can be miserable with them.

Once I'm home, I take a quick shower to freshen myself up. Bridge and Boh won't be here for about another hour, so I put a couple bottles of wine in the freezer, as I forgot to put them in the fridge this morning, and go put on a nice skater dress with tights. I don't need to dress up, but I don't want to look sluggish when they come around. I apply minimal makeup and clip my hair up out of my face while I cook dinner. I'm cooking a pesto chicken pasta dish from a recipe I found online, there are all types of herbs and spices in, but the sauce sounded amazing! It's a cheese sauce with wine, which I thought sounded strange but when I tried, it was delicious. It made me think of Jace straight away, he would have loved it.

I get the wine out of the freezer and pour myself a glass, then place the bottles in my fridge. It's 6:00 p.m., they should be here soon. As if they heard my thoughts, my buzzer goes off, and I run to the intercom, letting them up, then open my door. The elevator doors are opposite my apartment, so when it opens, I stand there with a large grin as Bridge and Boh come into view. Then everything stops. Cash is standing behind them, looking straight at me. *Did they say Cash was coming?*

"Rylee, my beautiful girl," Bridge says, taking my face in her hands and bringing me in for a tight hug. I peer over her shoulder at Boh grinning at me, obviously not realizing my shock. Cash is looking everywhere except at me. I don't mind him being here, but he always brings an air of tension with him and I can never relax. Also, after what happened those months ago and not hearing from him, it is awkward. I wonder if Bridge and Boh know. They haven't said anything.

I bring my attention back to Bridget. "Hi," I say, giving her a squeeze back. She lets go, walking inside, and Boh comes up to me next.

"Hey, Ry." He gives me a big squeeze that has my toes nearly leaving the floor as I try and get my hands around his broad frame. He lets go, then walks in the apartment behind Bridge.

Cash says, "Hi" while looking at the ground.

Normally, I can ignore awkwardness and act like things don't happen, but I have a feeling Cash will make that impossible. He pushes a bottle of white wine in front of me. I look down and it's my favorite sauvignon blanc. I look up at him.

"My favorite."

He looks me in the eye for the first time since being here. "I know. I hope you don't mind me coming. Bridge invited me. She said you would be fine with it, but judging by your face, I'm assuming you didn't know?" He winces. I take the bottle of wine from him and plaster on a smile.

"I didn't, but it's fine," I assure him. "There is plenty of food. I hope you like Italian." I smile at him, hoping he will push this tension aside, at least for tonight. To be honest, I should be embarrassed, he shouldn't feel any type of way. He helped me when I needed it. I don't know why he is acting weird.

"Sounds great." He nods with a slight smile. I take this as a win, and Cash follows me into the apartment, closing the door behind him.

"Rylee, this smells amazing!" Bridget beams at me as I walk in the kitchen, putting the wine in the fridge and pulling out the already open one I have.

"Wine?" I ask.

They all nod while I pour us a little in each glass. "Dinner will be ready any minute if you all want to take a seat. I will just put everything in dishes on the table and you can all help yourself, if that's okay?"

"Perfect, Ry," Boh says, heading into the dining room. I dish up the food and take it one by one to the table. I sit opposite Cash with Bridge to my right and Boh next to Cash, opposite Bridge.

Bridget picks up her glass. "To Jace," she says with unshed tears in her eyes.

"To Jace," we all say, raising our glasses. Cash's watery gaze meets mine briefly before we all take a sip of our wine and dig in.

Bridge tells us all about a new safari in South Africa she is thinking of going on. It sounds amazing, and when she shows us all the pictures, I'm instantly jealous. I contemplate telling them what I have decided, speaking of vacations.

"I'm going to go to the beach house," I fumble out way too quickly.

"The one Jace booked?" Cash injects.

I nod, taking a sip of my wine, contemplating how I make them understand why I want to go there on my own. "I think it will be good for me to go, on my own. I was going to cancel it, and I know I told you all I was, but the more I thought about it, I just couldn't." I look down at my plate, moving my food around with my fork. "Jace booked that place for a reason. Yes, he wanted us to go there," I say, blinking rapidly in the hope the tears don't fall. "But now he is not here, I feel it's only right I still go. He booked that with me in mind, I need to go spend the time there." I take another sip of the wine. "I may even feel closer to him."

Cash is side-eyeing me, and I know he is probably concerned because of what happened when he picked me up from the club, but I'm getting better. I will never forget Jace, but I know he would want me to live, and I know for a fact he would want me going to that beach house.

"I think it's a lovely idea, Ry," Boh says, and Bridge agrees. Cash stays silent, staring at the wineglass like it's about to come up with all the answers to life.

We continue chatting, and Bridge tells me we can go clothes shopping for vacation stuff before I go. I tell her I would like that and said we will book a time nearer the day. Once we have all finished with our food. I tell them I bought a shop-owned apple pie, as desserts are not my forte. I'm awful at them. They all laugh and say they will have some in a bit.

I go to stand up and clear the dishes away, but Bridge tells me to sit, and she will do it all. Boh stands up, offering her a hand, leaving Cash and me alone. I know he is going to mention the vacation, so I just wait. We sit in silence for what feels forever.

"Do you think going on the vacation is a good idea, Ry?" he asks while twirling the little bit of wine left in his glass.

"I know what you're thinking, but I'm in a better place now, Cash. I'm getting there, I promise."

Cash's eyes linger on me for what feels like forever but is probably only a few seconds. Then he just nods and excuses himself. I get up to go to the toilet and pop my head in the kitchen, and Bridge and Boh loading the dishwasher.

"Are you sure I can't help with anything?"

"No, you're good. Go put your feet up," Boh calls out.

I smile at him and then pop down the hallway to the bathroom. As I'm walking back to the dining room, I walk past Jace's office and the door is open. I keep the door shut at all times, so I know Cash must be in there or has been in there. I creep up peeking through the gap and see Cash sitting at Jace's desk with his head in his hands. I move to go in and see if he's okay and then stop when I hear his voice.

"I'm so sorry, son. I'm so, so sorry," he cries out. "I don't know how to make it stop, Jace."

Stop what? What is he talking about? I stand there for a few seconds, contemplating whether to go back to the dining room and pretend I didn't see Cash or go see what's wrong. I know if I go back, I won't be able to settle, and seeing him like this, sends a twinge to my heart. He has been there for me when I didn't even realize I needed him.

"Cash," I whisper, opening the door more so I can slip into the room. He wipes at his eyes hastily and stands up.

"Sorry. I was just . . . ahh!"

"There's nothing wrong with coming in here and talking to him, you know, Cash." He stays silent for a minute.

"I know." He sighs. "I just feel close to him in here."

"I get it." I don't say nothing else. I want to ask him what he meant when he was saying he doesn't know how to stop it but he's clearly upset right now. I don't want to intrude and tell him I was listening in on his moment.

"How do you do it, Rylee?" Cash asks, breaking the silence.

"Do what?" I say, staring at a photo of me and Jace he has sitting on his desk.

"Stay in this apartment. He is everywhere I look; I don't know how you do it."

I walk over to Jace's desk, picking up the picture and staring at it. It's when we were at Disney World in Florida the first year we met. I begged him to take a picture with Mickey Mouse and wear the ears, he protested for all of five minutes but then agreed. I was so happy I'm smiling like I'm on happy pills. Jace had said he had never seen me so happy; he wanted that memory forever and said he wanted my happiness looking back at him when he's having hard days at work, so he framed it and put it on his desk. I did, a couple of times, walk in on him holding the picture, staring at it with a smile on his face. I smile down at the picture.

"How could I leave this place. It's what keeps me going, Cash. I feel like I still have him here with me." I look up at him and give a half smile.

"That's not healthy though, is it?" He doesn't say it in a dick way, which is surprising for him. I know he's saying it in more of a caring way, and I get it. I agree with him to a certain extent, but this is my way of coping, and I feel like I'm getting there.

I shrug. "Maybe not." I place the picture back down and turn around to him. "But it's my way, and I like it this way."

I walk past him and open the door for me to slip out. Before I slip out of the room, I turn around to Cash.

"If you still have your key, you're more than welcome to come around whenever you want. Jace's memory will live here forever." I then slip out of the room, leaving him alone to have his moment in Jace's office.

Chapter 29

Later that night, once everyone has left, I do what I do every night. I lie in bed and cry in one of Jace's shirts. I know people would say I need to speak to someone or see someone but I'm content being like this. I know it's weird, but it feels like one of the only things getting me through. As my tears subside, I lie there in silence, waiting for the exhaustion to take me from crying so much.

I sit up in bed, thinking I heard something. It's dead silent, so I lie back down.

Bang. "Ahhh." I hear a manly groan.

I shoot up again. *What. The. Fuck.* Someone is in my apartment. My adrenaline kicks in as I hunt my room for something, anything to whack this person over the head with. *What if there is more than one?* It takes me a second to realize I should have probably called the cops. I look but then remember I left my phone on the dining room table from earlier. *Fuck.* I'm struggling to find anything, so I unplug my lamp and creep out. I don't know whether to go to the dining room or confront the person. As I get to my door, I hear a shuffle in the room next to mine. Jace's office. Oh my God. No way is anyone taking anything from there. Before I can even think, I'm charging out of my room and heading straight for the wide open office door. The figure is standing in front of the door. I don't think, I just swing the lamp as hard as I can, which is probably not even that hard, but it sends the person to the ground.

"Ahhh," they groan out. I turn the light on and am horrified to see Cash lying on the floor rolling around in pain.

"Oh my God," I shriek. "Cash!" I drop down to the floor, trying to get him to hold still.

"Cash, stop. Where are you hurt?" I say in a panic. Fuck, I don't even know where I hit him, it was too dark.

He's rubbing the bottom of his head aggressively, probably trying to damp down the pain. I go to touch the back of his head, but he pushes my hand away.

"Just let me look." I sigh. I still don't get what he is doing here in the middle of the night. Well, I can guess now that I'm getting a stench of alcohol off him. He moves his hand, allowing me to look. There is no blood, thank God, just a slight red mark.

"Do you feel dizzy or sick?"

"No," he grunts, trying to stand up. I help him up and he just stands there, well, tries but sways a little. I'm not sure if that's from the hit on the head or the alcohol. I move him over to Jace's desk chair and sit him down.

"Do you want to tell me what you were doing creeping in my apartment at 1:00 a.m.?"

"You should really be trying to ring the police when you think someone has broken in, not approach them, Rylee," he grumbles.

"Don't try and change the subject, what were you doing?"

"You ssssaid I could commmme whennnhever I wanted."

"I did. At a reasonable hour, Cash. Not in the middle of the night, scaring the shit out of me."

"I'm sorry." He goes to stand but wobbles slightly on his feet.

"Sit down, let me get you some water." I walk out of the room, heading for the kitchen. He has clearly been drinking and thoughts of Jace have invaded him, he wanted to be close to him, and I get it, his office does make you feel close to him. He spent a lot of his time in there and it still looks the exact same. I don't blame him; I just wish he wouldn't scare me at stupid o'clock in the morning. I grab a cold bottle of water out of the fridge and two painkillers from the cabinet. When I enter Jace's office, he has the picture of Jace and me in his hand, staring at it. I take the picture out of his hand, placing it back on the desk and pass him the bottle of water along with the two painkillers.

"Here." He takes both pills together and downs the bottle of water in a few gulps.

"Thanks." He places the empty bottle on Jace's desk and goes to stand.

"Stay seated for a bit," I tell him. I stand up, walking around him, checking the back of his head. It's red but there is no lump, so it should be okay. I'm still worried. I then realize with everything that has gone on, I totally forgot about Becky. She hasn't been mentioned since the night of his dinner.

"What happened with Becky?" I ask, filling the silence.

Cash shrugs. "Not much."

"Well, you seemed happy at your dinner, I thought she might have been the one."

He huffs a laugh out to that.

"What's funny about that?" I ask, confused at his reaction to my question.

"She was never the one, I don't think any woman will ever be the one, Ry. I don't deserve to be happy." He sighs, rubbing his hands over his face.

"What? Why don't you deserve to be happy?"

"Because I don't, just leave it." He raises his voice slightly, and I can tell I'm getting him agitated, pushing his buttons. Normally I wouldn't want to argue with Cash, but something comes over me and makes me want to push his buttons more. I want to know why he doesn't deserve to be happy.

"No, I won't leave it," I deadpan. "C'mon, tell me. Why don't you deserve it?"

"Because I'm a piece of shit, I'm a shit person, a shit boss, and even worse father." He pauses. "Was a shit father," he whispers, glancing back up at the picture of Jace and me. Before I can question him further, he continues. "I didn't deserve such an amazing son, Ry. I did the worst thing a father could do, and I'll never forgive myself."

Now I'm really curious as to what he is going on about. Jace never said anything bad about Cash. If anything, he always stuck up for him. When Cash told me about what happened with Jace's mom, I thought it maybe had to do with the fact he raised Jace on his own, but he was thankful to his dad for that and rightly so, but what he is saying now has me questioning everything. *What did he do?*

"Wh-what are you talking about, Cash?" A part of me wants to know but another part is worried about what he will tell me.

I crouch down in front of him, coming face-to-face with him. His whiskey-ridden breath floats out from his open lips. I survey his face while he does the same to me. *What is he hiding?*

"I felt things I shouldn't have, Ry," he whispers. He doesn't take his eyes off me, roaming my face like it's the first time he's really seeing me. I should feel slightly uncomfortable in this moment, with how close we are, but strangely enough, I don't.

"What things?" I ask. I don't think I can let this go. I need to know what's going on, and now I'm wondering if this is what has caused him to act the way he does toward me. Even though I have no idea what he is talking about.

"It doesn't matter." He shakes his head, breaking the stare between us. He goes to stand up again, but I push myself forward, pushing him back down on the seat.

"No!" I raise my voice slightly. "Tell me, if you were this huge shitty person and such a bad dad, then tell me, Cash. Jace isn't here to judge you now, is he? So tell me." It's a low blow, rubbing what he already knows in his face. He winced when I said it, and it makes me feel like shit, but he can't say that and expect me to forget about it.

He gets close to my face, and the smell of whiskey permeates the air.

"If you found out, you would think I was the biggest piece of shit too, Rylee. If anything, it might even be better that way, I have tried to make it this way for years." He stands, which causes me to fall back. *What the hell is he going on about?* I stand up, rushing after him.

"No, you can't just say this and not explain, Cash. What are you talking about? I already think you're a piece of a shit, so it won't make me think any less of you." Again, I'm going in deep, I feel the more I wind Cash up, the more he reacts, then the more he will say. I do think he's a piece of shit, sometimes, but not all the time. He just clearly has issues, issues I want to know about. He is walking toward the door, so I run around him, standing in front of him, blocking the door.

"Tell me." I stare anxiously into his eyes. "Please."

He takes two strides toward me, now only centimeters away from me, which causes me to have to look up at him. His warm whiskey breath fans my face, and his eyes look wild with anger, frustration, and something else I can't quite determine.

"You need to stay away from me, Rylee," he grinds out.

"Why," I breathe out, glaring at him. He stares down at me as we stand toe to toe, his broad chest grazing my nipples only covered by the thin layer of Jace's sweatshirt. My nipples pebble as he takes deeper breaths, causing his chest to rub against them more. I blush as his eyes drift down and sweep over my chest. I close my eyes, mortified that he has seen. I don't think I can face him after this, it has to be an automatic reaction. When I open my eyes seconds later, the blue is nowhere to be seen in Cash's eyes, they are blown wide, swimming with heat. My breath hitches, my body temperature skyrocketing. *What the hell is happening to me?*

He leans down, his lips grazing my ear. "Because I don't have the strength to stay away from you anymore . . . that's why," he whispers before placing his hand on the handle and opening the door, causing me to stumble to the side. He brushes past me, leaving the apartment. I stand there in shock as he leaves and doesn't look back. He takes the stairs, soon to be out of sight. I continue to stare at the stairs. The words replaying over and over in my head. *"Because I can't stay away from you."* My mind knows what he means, but I'm struggling to accept it. *Cash wants me?* I close the door and turn, and I slide down to the floor, still in shock. Everything floods my memory of earlier when he was in the office, him saying sorry to Jace, him saying he couldn't make it stop. He was talking about me.

Chapter 30

I arrived at the office at six this morning. It's now nearly 9:00 a.m. and I still haven't turned the laptop on. Guzzling my third cup of extra strong coffee, which isn't even touching the exhaustion I feel, I turn the laptop on, hoping work will take my mind off everything that happened last night. I tossed and turned all night, and eventually slipped into a sleep around 4:00 a.m.

I wish I hadn't. That was the first night I went to sleep without a single tear because I was too busy thinking about what had happened between Cash and me. I even waited in Jace's t-shirt for them to come but they didn't. *Is this what people talk about when they say it gets easier?* Instead, I had lain there, thinking of Cash who then assaulted my dreams. I woke up hot, sweating and crying from utter guilt at the thoughts I had about Cash. *How can this be happening?* I have never looked at Cash in that way. Yes, he is gorgeous, but he is Jace's dad. He is my dead boyfriend's dad, who has been a complete asshole to me for the last five years. I place my elbows on the desk, dropping my head into my hands, rubbing at my face in the hope this will wash away everything that has happened in the last twelve hours.

"Oh no, what's happened, Ry?" Rachel's gentle voice interrupts my internal meltdown. My head lulls back, and I gaze into her worried eyes, and everything floods out of me through tears.

"Oh, baby, come here." Rach rushes around my desk, grabbing me in a tight hug, rocking me back and forth while I unload all my guilt tears. The thing that hurts the most is that she automatically thinks I'm crying because of Jace. Although I'm crying over the guilt, I'm crying because I haven't stopped thinking about Cash, and every time I replay those words "*Because I can't stay away from you*," I get the slightest of butterflies. *Why!* This shouldn't be happening. I don't tell Rachel what happened. I know she won't judge—also I haven't actually done anything wrong—but my thoughts are filling me with guilt. Could it be the fact I'm lonely and Cash can relate to my grief? I never thought of him in that way until he said those words to me. *Why did he have to say that?*

"Why don't you go home, Ry?" Rach suggests, leaning back and wiping my tear-stained cheeks.

I shake my head. "I think that will be the worse thing for me." She nods, as if understanding why I don't want to be on my own, probably thinking I will just sit there thinking of Jace, when it will no doubt be his dad. The thought makes me sick to my stomach.

"How about this, then, when we finish up here for the day, we go out for some drinks after work? I think some of the others are going too, or we can go out just us?"

I raise my eyebrow at her. "And is Harley going?"

"There she is, always calling me out." She rolls her eyes while laughing.

"We need to catch up on this. I haven't forgotten."

"And that is my cue," she singsongs while walking toward my office door. "Make sure you are logged off that laptop at five thirty, sharp, Ms. Matthews!" she says, shutting the door behind her.

My day went better than I thought it would, it was busy which kept my mind off things. Five thirty is fast approaching as I finish my last email for the day. I'm looking forward to getting out with the group tonight, it's been a long time since I have been out with work friends. I press send on my last email, closing the laptop. I grab my bag and touch up on my makeup, making sure I look half presentable and not dead like I feel inside.

Rach pops her head through my door. "You ready?"

I nod. "Yep, coming."

As I walk out of my office, Rachel takes my hand in hers.

"You sure you're okay with coming out tonight with the guys? We can go out, just us two, and put the world to rights?" She flashes me a soft smile.

"As tempting as that sounds, I think a night out with everyone is what I need."

"Okay, if you're sure." She squeezes my hand before letting go.

"Rylee!" Harley shouts as we make our way outside where everyone is waiting for a taxi. Everyone turns to me with huge smiles, showing how excited they are to see me. I know from this that I made the right decision coming out.

We all gather in three cabs, heading to O'Neill's for some drinks. Everyone is busy talking in the cab while I take in all the lights as we pass, watching the busy world go by and everyone looking ecstatic it's Friday and they have no work tomorrow. Before I know it, we are pulling up outside O'Neill's. I jump out and Rach follows me, and we head inside. It's a large bar, with gentle music playing in the background, it's busy in here tonight, as we have to squeeze through a bunch of people to get to the bar. Rach gets there first, ordering drinks for us as she shouts back at everyone, asking what they want. She doesn't ask me, so I'm assuming she will know to order me a wine. As I expect, Rach turns around with a cold glass of white wine, which I eagerly grab and take a large gulp. I sigh as I swallow.

"You look like you needed that," a voice I know injects from behind me. I spin around, surprised to see James.

"James!"

He smiles at me, pointing to my wine. "Long week?"

I roll my eyes at him while taking another gulp of the wine. "You have no idea."

He chuckles to himself. "I know the feeling, so who are you here with tonight, then?" he asks.

I look around and point out as many people as I can see. "I'm just out with work for a few. What about you?" I look behind him, not seeing anyone.

"Just on my own, thought I would pop in for a quick one before going home." He smiles, raising his empty beer glass.

"Let me get you another, I owe you a coffee from the other day," I mention, which then makes me think of Cash, who I'm meant to not be thinking about.

"You sure?" he questions. "I don't want to take you away from your colleagues."

I wave him off. "Don't be silly, you can join us if you want?" I say, pointing behind me to everyone.

He flashes an eager smile at me, nodding. "Yeah, I would like that."

I smile at him while pushing myself through people to get to the bar. I wave a bartender down and order myself and Rach another glass of wine and James a beer, automatically ordering him what I would order for Jace. A lump forms in my throat as they pass me the beer and I pass it back to James.

"I'm sorry, I hope you're okay with Blue Moon, it's what—"

"Jace always drank." James finishes my sentence while taking the beer from me. "Where do you think he got his good taste in beer from?" James winks, easing the tension.

I laugh and turn around, grabbing mine and Rach's wine.

"Respectfully, James. It tastes like ass, so it's nothing to be proud off." He throws his head back on a laugh and follows me, squeezing through people to find Rach. When we find her, I smile at her, and hand over a glass of wine. She downs the glass she had in her hand and thanks me for the next one. I have a feeling she will get wasted tonight.

"This is James," I say to Rach and a few others standing near. "He is one of Jace's friends." The guys walk over, shaking his hand and introducing themselves.

The night took a turn. Three hours later and Rach and I have moved from wine to tequila. The minute I yawned, Rach was having none of it and told me I needed to stay out with them, so she brought out the hard stuff. I'm pleased I stayed out, this is just what I needed—a good, relaxed night with friends in a great bar. James has fit in well and is now playing pool with the guys.

Rach and I walk over. "I will play the winner," I state to James and Harley. It looks like I will be playing Harley, James is doing terrible and has potted hardly any of his balls.

I raise my eyebrow at James as he scratches his head while laughing.

"Hey, it's been a while since I have shot pool." He tries to defend his shocking playing after he hit the cue ball and doesn't hit any of his balls, which then gives Harley two shots. Harley only had one of his balls left and then the eight ball, which he pockets with ease.

I take over and play Harley. I do much better than James. The score is even. James has even been trying to put me off all game, knocking me as I go to shoot, telling god-awful jokes, making me laugh. I don't think he can stand knowing I will beat Harley and he couldn't. It has come down to the eight ball left. It's my turn but the ball is in a very awkward position. I'm walking around the table, taking this seriously. I used to love playing pool with Jace, and I always wanted to win. I'm pretty sure he used to let me win most of the time. James comes up behind me as I bend down.

"I would go with the way you were going to go before," he whispers into my ear, placing his hand on my hip. It causes me to freeze slightly but I know the touch is completely innocent. Before I can reply, I'm interupputed.

"Get your fucking hands off her before I remove them myself." I spin around in shock to see who the person is speaking to and am floored to see it's Cash and he's glaring at James, who slowly pulls his hand away.

"Cash," I scold him. I can't believe he said that in front of everyone. I look around, and everyone is staring between Cash, James, and me, waiting to see what happens. My cheeks redden in embarrassment.

"Don't even go there, Rylee. Moving on from my son already is bad enough but with one of his piece-of-shit ex-friends? That's low, even for you." Gasps come from behind me.

"You don't fucking speak to her like that." James has taken three strides to Cash, pointing in his face. Cash's and James's chests flare up, and they're standing toe to toe. Cash has a good five inches on James and about fifty pounds in pure muscles, but this doesn't make James step back.

"And what are you going to do about it, pussy boy?" Cash spits.

Before I can see or hear anymore, I turn around, grabbing my bag. I can't even say anything to Cash, I'm so embarrassed and angry with what he said in front of everyone. Luckily, I know most of them but some I don't, and he has gone and made me out to be some cheap tart who goes chasing Jace's friends.

Rach runs around the side of the pool table towards me. She looks at me, shaking her head, her brows raised, her eyes wide.

"I'm sure he didn't mean it, Ry."

I shake my head back and forth. "I don't care, I can't do this. I'm out of here." As I walk away, James calls my name. I don't turn around, I pull my phone out of my pocket, ordering an Uber, which thankfully is two minutes away. I need to get out of here, the tears are already falling down my face from the utter embarrassment. I push the door open, the cool breeze hits my face, making me feel slightly more drunk than I did two seconds ago. I look down at my phone, which says my car is here. I look back up and the car pulls up right in front of me. I jump in and as the driver goes to pull off, the passenger door opens and a large frame drops into the seat. When Cash turns around with utter rage in his eyes, it makes me realize how ready I am to have this long overdue showdown with him. I'm done with letting him treat me like shit, it stops now.

Chapter 31

I'm marching through my apartment, ready to have this showdown with Cash, once and for all. I told him in the Uber I would not embarrass myself any more by having a full-on argument with him in the back seat. We sat in silence the whole way; I wouldn't be surprised if the Uber driver didn't feel the rage brewing between Cash and me.

I have always held back with him, but I'm done. He confused the hell out of me last night. I have told myself all day it was the grief, and Cash was someone I could relate to, but something in the pit of my stomach was saying otherwise. I needed to go out tonight to forget what had happened, to stop my mind going into overdrive about Cash and the things he admitted, but, of course, he had to turn up and ruin everything, throw his asshole self around. Cash made me feel a millimeter tall tonight; he embarrassed me unlike anyone ever has. He made me feel ashamed and like I was doing something wrong.

My apartment door slams, so I spin around, ready to go at him. "How dare you, you fucking hypocrite," I scream, projecting every bit of anger I have toward him. When I thought back to what he said in the bar and then what he had all but admitted last night, it made me realize how much of a hypocrite he actually is.

He drops his head back, chuckling to himself. "How dare I?" He points to himself and then switches his finger to point at me. "How dare you," he grits out, ignoring the hypocrite remark. *Surprise, surprise.* "You were all over James like a fucking rash tonight, I was there a lot longer than you think. I was watching you, all the little touches, the laughing. No longer upset about my dead son, are you?"

Two steps and I slap Cash in the face harder than I think I have ever slapped anyone in my life. The red mark is instant and proof of that, as well as the throbbing in my palm. It's a good pain though, it felt good. He doesn't even react to the slap; his face stays the same. Anger, sadness. Something else I can't quite decipher. "Fuck you and get the fuck out of my apartment." I point to the door over his shoulder. I spin around, heading for the kitchen. I need a drink, or twenty.

"Why that slimy fucking prick, Rylee?" I roll my eyes before turning back to Cash. If he won't leave, I'll make him.

"Because he's great in bed, that's why, Cash. He makes me forget." I struggle holding the vomit down even saying it. Is it true? Fuck no. I have only hugged James, that's as far as he has ever gotten. I just need Cash out of this house and away from me. I can't have him around me, and as much as I know he's here for Jace, a part of me feels that's not the only reason.

Right in front of my eyes, it's like a mask being slipped on Cash's face, the anger that takes over is not something I have seen on him before.

"Say that again, I dare you," he grits out, taking two colossal steps toward me. Now standing directly in front of me, I can feel his harsh breaths on my face. He's transforming right before my eyes. I have never seen this side of him before. He's raging so hard a blood vessel might pop in his eye.

I straighten and push my shoulders back, locking eyes with him. "Because he's great in—"

Cash grabs my neck in a harsh grip, pulling me forward, and his mouth crashes into mine, almost hurting with his forcefulness. It knocks me back, but before I can fall, Cash grips me around the waist, pulling me closer to him. My head is screaming for me to pull away, but I don't. I push back into Cash, channeling my anger and frustration for him through our kiss. His tongue meets mine as we overpower one another. He pulls away, and instantly I feel the loss. I look at him, waiting for him to freak out, even waiting for me to freak out but we don't. Cash looks at me like he wants to eat me whole.

"You taste like every bad decision, just as I thought you would," he rasps against my lips.

"Clearly, bad decisions are your favorite pastime," I tease back. *Why? I don't know.* He made me mad tonight, and with the alcohol mixed in with my anger, another side of me is coming out.

He crashes his mouth to mine again, grabbing me by the nape of my neck, walking me backward toward the couch. The backs of my knees meet the softness of the couch as he pushes me down with force. I fall on the cushions. Cash doesn't give me a minute, he's on me, caging me between his large arms, his tongue dancing with mine. He's right, the taste is like a bad decision, but a bad decision I never knew I wanted to make. I crave it. Our tongues keep dancing with each other, our teeth clashing together from the force.

The kiss sends a feeling surging through me, a feeling I never thought I would feel again. I lie there beneath him, weak and confused. Cash Stiles wasn't meant to make me feel this way. My legs open wider. I don't know why, I just need to feel something, feel him. Cash's body falls closer to mine and then his hard dick presses against me. He groans into my mouth as he pushes harder into my center. I push up, shamelessly rubbing myself on him, the ache that forms in the pit of my stomach flows through me like a tidal wave. It's as if a switch goes off in our minds at the same time, and we both freeze, and Cash pulls his lips away from mine. His gaze drops from my eyes to my mouth and back up again. He looks pained and I know it is mirrored by me. The sickness settles in thick and fast.

"We should stop, Ry," he rasps out. His brows drawn together as he drops his chin to his chest.

I nod as tears well in my eyes. The shame, the embarrassment, but most of all, the guilt for how much I wanted Cash, for how much I still do. Cash lifts off me and sits beside me on the sofa, rubbing his hands through his hair. When he looks up, he stares straight ahead at something in front him. I follow his line of sight and he's studying a picture of Jace and me. With the guilt I'm feeling, I can only imagine it's ten times stronger for him.

"I want to say sorry, but I can't." He sighs, still staring at the picture. I stay seated in silence, speechless. I don't know what else to say, I have nothing to say.

"Saying sorry would mean I didn't mean it, or I regret it, and I probably should, but I don't." He turns around to me.

"You're ingrained in me, Rylee. I don't want you there, but you are. I think you always have been." He drops his head, looking down at his hands.

"Even when you belonged to my son," he whispers, as if he can't believe he is saying it out loud. He sighs, standing up and turning to me.

"I'll leave you, but if you need me, please call, and don't you dare feel any guilt about what just happened, it was all me, but I'm not saying sorry, Ry."

"I don't want you to be sorry," I rush out before I can even think about it, as much as I should want him to, as much as I should be sorry, I'm not. I have never met someone who makes me so angry and frustrated, but, at the same time, there is some kind of invisible magnet pulling me to him, making me want him more, it overpowers the anger I have toward him.

He nods. "I'm going to head off, I don't think staying here any longer is going to do us any favors."

I agree with him. It won't. Cash set off a feeling in me I never thought I would feel again, even if it was just a sliver, and I know the longer he is here, the more I will want it back. I wrap my arms around myself, nodding back to him, not trusting myself to speak. If I do, I will beg him to stay. He walks toward me, placing a kiss on my forehead. I let out a breath I didn't realize I was holding.

"Oh, and Ry." I turn to the door, seeing him standing there with the front door open. He looks over his shoulder. "I know I was an asshole and a hypocrite tonight, and I am sorry for that, I truly am, but please trust me when I tell you to stay away from James, I don't trust him."

"Okay." I know something has gone on, but I don't push. As much as I hate doing what anyone tells me, especially Cash, I can tell he's asking in a pleading way, so for now, I will accept it and leave it. I want to know what has happened, but now is not the time. He smiles, walking out the door and closing it behind him.

I walk back to the sofa, dropping myself down, gazing up at the ceiling. How did my night go from me having fun with my colleagues and James, to being humiliated in front of them, to coming back to my apartment and nearly having sex with the person who humiliated me—the love of my life's dad? If I thought life couldn't get any more complicated, Cash fucking Stiles charges in like a bulldozer, taking down the wall I had built around me and whatever is left of me along with it. I close my eyes and let out a big sigh, the fatigue settling in. I close my eyes, and all that replays is Cash's lips on mine. *I'm so fucked.*

Chapter 32

My toes sink into the sand beneath my feet. I look up at the waves, watching them crash against each other. I have been coming here every few weeks, mostly to think, but I also like coming here to speak to Jace. It's my way of coping, if you can call it that.

The beach was mine and Jace's favorite place. We always said that when we grew old and gray together, we would get a beach house and spend the rest of our days happy on the sand and near the sea. It guts me to the core to know I will never get that with him. The only person I ever wanted it with.

I lie down on the sand, gazing up at the sky. Jace is up there right now. I wonder if he's watching me, is he happy or angry. He would have every right to be angry after what happened three nights ago. This is why I needed to come here today. Like I needed to explain myself, but how can I? I rub at the pendant around my neck. Bridget bought me a heart-shaped pendant that has what looks like blue and gray specks inside. When Bridget told me its Jace's ashes that have been made into glass, I broke down, clutching the necklace with everything I had. I put it on that day and haven't taken it off since. I always hold the necklace; it makes me feel closer to him.

"Jace," I say, continuing my gaze up at the clouds. "Where do I even start?" I sigh. I'm running my fingers through the sand next to me, trying to ground my anxiousness.

"I miss you. I have missed talking to you. I just needed some time to get my head together, although it still isn't, if anything, it's even more messed up." With the wind lapping around my head, it's like I can feel Jace running his fingers through my hair, like the way he used to always do when I was anxious.

"I'm sorry it took me so long." I laugh. I sit in silence for a minute. There is so much to say, but I'm struggling to find the words, so I start with the obvious. "I'm sorry, Jace. I'm so sorry," I whisper, taking a deep breath. "I don't know why it happened or how. All I know is I have never wanted it before, never once have I ever looked at your dad like that. I hated him and now . . ." I take a minute to gather my thoughts. "The hate has gone." I sigh "After the kiss, I felt something. I felt a piece of myself come back, a piece of life, Jace. I haven't felt like that since you were here." Tears fall down the sides of my face as I cry to the sky, to Jace. "I'm sorry, I'm here talking to you about this. I need you to forgive me, Jace. I just need a sign that you forgive me."

I lie there for what feels like forever, listening to the waves and the seagulls, waiting for that sign but it doesn't come. It starts to get dark, and I know I need to go, but I'm holding on for that sign. It's then I hear the rumbling. I sit up, looking out to the ocean, and black clouds appear with what looks like is a storm heading toward shore in May—this never happens.

Jace hated storms.

He doesn't forgive me.

I lie in the rain, still not moving from where I was talking to Jace. I deserve to stay in the rain, the miserable rain that he sent me. I know people will think I'm being silly coming to the beach and talking to him and assuming that a storm is his way of saying he doesn't forgive me, but in a weird way, it's what I need. I need to cling onto that fact that he listens when I need to talk to him and ask advice or tell him things, I did wrong. I want reactions out of him, I want him to be angry with me, I'm angry with myself, I deserve this.

My thoughts are interrupted when my phone vibrates against my leg. I pick up my bag and dig through to find the phone. When I find it, I sigh. It's Cash. I can't talk to him right now. I told him I needed time away from him and to just leave me alone for a while. I needed to sort my head out. I don't know what I'm feeling. I know his head is as messed up as mine. He lost his son, and I can't imagine how it must feel to lose an only child. I keep telling myself we are both grieving and finding comfort in each other because we loved Jace so much, so it makes us feel closer to him, but deep down, I know it's not that, but I can't bring myself to say what I know out loud. It's so much more than that, and it terrifies me.

My phone vibrates again. I sit there and watch it ring. I'm too tired for this, especially after today. I thought coming here would help, but it has made me feel like an even trashier human. I look at my phone and a text has come through from Cash.

> Cash: It's urgent, I really need to speak to you. Pick up your phone.

What is that about? Sighing, I get up from where I am, heavier than before, due to how wet I am from the rain. I try dusting off the sand that has stuck to my clothes and skin as best as I can and then I walk back to the car. I'll call Cash, hands-free, on the way home. I'm sure he can wait five minutes. The darkness has come quickly, leaving a chill in the air, which I feel more now that I'm wet. I need to go home and have a nice hot bubble bath and try to relax. I need to fix my head. I know people are worried about me, but it takes so much of my energy to be fake and put a smile on. I would rather be sad and people just leave me to being sad. I'm allowed to be sad; people seem to forget this.

As I get nearer to the parking lot, I stop and turn around, looking at the view. There's lightning in the distance, flashing off the ripples of the water. To be honest, I picked this beach because I know few people come here, and I wanted to be completely on my own with my thoughts . . . and Jace.

As I approach my car, I jump out of my skin as I hear a loud bang. I spin around and see a bin laying on the ground, the wind picking up. Holding my chest, while my heart beats erratically,

I take deep breaths to calm myself. I dig through my bag to get my keys out. It's then I hear what sounds like heavy breathing. *What the—*

An arm comes from behind me, wrapping around my upper body, and they hold my back flush against their front. I freeze up and before I can scream, a cloth is placed over my nose and mouth, a little room is left for me to breathe but then my body gets weak. My vision blurs and my body goes numb, and as tears fall, I realize there is no way out of this, pins and needles fill my whole body as I become weaker and weaker. My head spins as someone lifts me, throwing me over their shoulder. I lift my head and the outline of my car gets farther and farther away.

"Help me," I barely whisper as the darkness takes me under.

Chapter 33

I open my eyes slowly; my head is pounding and my whole body aches. *What the hell happened*? I lift my head, and a shooting pain that would put a migraine to shame courses through me. I wince, trying to look around the room, having to shut one eye. I drop my head back down, landing on soft pillows. *My head hurts so much.* I take a few deep breaths and try raising my head again. I open my eyes again, and I can see more clearly now. The pain is still destroying me, but I need to know what the fuck is going on, so I try and forget about the pain for a couple of minutes.

I look around, this place is massive. *Where the hell am I?* Panic settles in thick and fast, and it's then I let out a gasp as everything hits me like a freight train. The beach, the parking lot, someone coming up from behind me. Oh my God. I bring my hands to my mouth, letting out a huge sob. I'm sick with fear, someone has kidnapped me. *Who would want to do that?* I haven't done anything. I drop my head, sobbing and letting the pain from my head tear through me. *What if they kill me?* I close my eyes and think of Jace to calm me, he always calmed me, but it's not Jace's face I see, it's Cash. Cash's face makes me curl up in a ball and cry until it lulls me into the darkness again.

Opening my eyes, I get ready for the pain from earlier to assault my head, thankfully, it has settled. I don't know how long I slept for, there are no windows in here, but there are lights that seem to have stayed on. I slowly sit up and take a good look around. I'm lying on a single bed with fluffy pillows and a big fluffy duvet. I'm so confused. *What the fuck is going on right now?*

I cast my eyes around the room again; I can only describe this as what used to be a barn but has been converted. The ceilings are extremely tall with wooden beams going all the way across. I follow the beams down the room, it feels like it goes on forever. There is not much in here, which makes it look even bigger. I slowly drop my feet off the bed, standing up, thinking maybe I can get out of here somehow. It's then I notice there is a table at the end of the bed with a container and a bottle of water. Seeing the water makes me realize how thirsty I am, so I grab the water, which is sealed. If it hadn't been, there is no way I would be drinking it. I take a few gulps, drinking half of the bottle. I place the bottle back down, eyeing up the black container. I open it up and am shocked to see a sandwich. *What kind of kidnapper puts a sandwich in a black container?* Even looking at it makes me feel sick. I close the lid.

Scanning the room again, and I spot a large wooden door at the end. Knowing this will be my way out, I rush toward it, filling myself with hope the nearer I get. I pull on the handle, but the door's locked. Of course it is. I continue and see a door at the other end, so I rush toward it, I don't know why I think they will be unlocked, but I have to try. It, of course, is also locked.

I sigh, peering around the room, there must be something. I pace up and down what feels like for hours but is probably no longer than five minutes. There is nothing, no windows, the doors are locked, and after banging on them for a while, there is no way I could break through them; they are solid. I drop to my knees, realizing there is no hope. *How long will I be here for? What does this person want with me?* Then I just lose it, I scream and scream at the top of my lungs.

"Help me, someone please help me, please," I choke out on a sob. I don't know what to do, I'm so scared. After everything that has happened to me, why this, why now? What even do they want with me?

A noise comes from behind me, and I tense up, but I'm too petrified to turn around. My whole body is shaking while I'm trying not to breathe, in the hopes that whoever it is will go away.

"No one is coming for you, Rylee." Everything around me starts spinning. That voice. I know that voice, it takes me a minute to place it. *It can't be, please no.*

I slowly turn on my hands and knees, staring down at the floor, unable to bring myself to look up.

"It's been a long six years, and I have been patient enough, but you're right where you belong now, with me. Like you always should have been." The voice drips with venom.

Tears run down my face as I prepare for what is going to break me even more than I already am. Pain and confusion is all I feel right now.

I look up staring into those pitch-black eyes.

"Hi, Rylee." He smugly smiles at me, leaning against the wooden door.

Gasping, my hand flies to my mouth, hoping that will keep the vomit at bay. This can't be happening. Tears are streaming as I shake my head back and forth.

"No, No . . ."

Praying that my eyes are playing tricks on me, I wipe at them but he's still there. Still watching me like he is eating away at my soul.

"James."

TO BE CONTINUED...

Afterword

I know that some of you will be feeling slightly angry and upset with how this storyline went. It was the book, not only that I wanted to write, but needed to. Yes, these books are fiction and there is a lot of fictional scenarios in this story, however, I wanted to also bring realism into this story. The story behind the story is that, the people we love with everything can be there one day and then gone the next and there's nothing, sadly, we can do about that. So, hold onto them with everything and always show and tell them, how much they mean to you.

Acknowledgments

TO MY READERS – I want to thank you so much for taking the time to read my baby! I know this is not what people expected and I am sorry for that, I cannot tell you how much it gutted me to write this storyline- I cried for days! Jace was one of the most precious souls ever, he literally is my dream man and to lose him like that, honestly killed a part of me. Jace Stiles will always and forever hold a place in my heart. I hope you stay with me on this. There are not enough words to explain how much I truly do appreciate you all, so please stalk me, message me and tell me how much you hate me because I will do everything I can to make you love me again – I promise!

TONI - (Yes she is real!!! However, Toni in Always. Forever's. personality is fictional – mostly LOL) – My best friend, my soul sister, and my Alpha/proof-reader LOL. You were more excited than me when I told you everything was coming together, when I sent you my book cover, when I put my pre-order up, you literally screamed down the phone to me with excitement and you didn't stop asking how the book was going, even when I was struggling, you made it a big deal and that is what I needed because you were my inner voice and I love you like you wouldn't believe. I know I don't tell or show you enough my baby, but you are literally my right arm, Ton and I don't know where I would be without you. Thank you for being you, never change.

KB.ROW & KAYLEIGH – My besties for life! The fact we met over our love for books just shows we were meant to be, and I don't know how I went through 27 odd years without you both in it! I love you both so, sooo much. We are the ultimate trio and no one can tell me different. You are my favourite bitches to be bitches with.

KB – You were the one that told me I could do this, and I honestly don't think I would have opened that google doc and started writing if it wasn't for you. Thank you for listening and helping me anytime I asked and, mostly, thank you for believing in me and pushing me to start this story. The early stages, I struggled big time and talking out loud to you about the storyline helped so much. I also need to say another thank you for helping me with the formatting software, I NEVER would have been able to do that without you, you are the queen!

VEE & GEE – The troublesome twosomes and blurb queens. You're both simply the best, and I'm so thankful for you both, for helping me with my blurb and whenever I have had any questions you have always been there to help me. Vee, I have to give you a special shoutout for being the best hype girl on this planet, anyone would be lucky to have you on their team and, of course, as a best friend - I'm not letting you go. Keep being dramatic and and keep spiralling. I love you both so much, never leave me, OK?– thanks.

LAURA – We started this journey together and I cannot wait to continue this journey with you and watch you grow. I'm so lucky to have met you through bookstagram and now can call you my friend. Thank you for all the help and being there when I have needed to rant! I love you.

RHIANNON & TASH (Well, who I like to call, dick-pic Tash LOL) – You are both the best hype girls and have given me amazing support. You're both generally amazing friends and I am so grateful bookstagram brought me the both of you. I appreciate and love you both so much.

DEE – Thank you for being such an amazing editor, your strengthened this book so much. I cannot explain to you how thankful I am. I'm lucky to have you.

TO MY MUM – I would do anything to have you here and to be reading this, I can hear your voice telling me how proud you are of me and writing this book was the outlet I needed. You will live in my heart, Always and Forever. Rest in perfect peace my angel.

Also By PS Black

Lost & Found Duet

Always. Forever.

Make Me Feel Again

About Author

I'm a South London, UK girl through and through that says "innit" far too many times. I moved to Norfolk, UK around six years ago which was a huge change, but I love the peacefulness! When I'm not writing, you can find me reading a book (Massive lover of MM, Taboo and Age Gap), eating hella chocolate or just perving over my favourite book boyfriend.

You can find me on the below platforms:

Instagram – @Authorps.black

Facebook – PS Black

TikTok – @Authorps.black

Join my Facebook reader group, PS Black's Sad Girl Club, for sneak peaks and info on upcoming books.

Printed in Great Britain
by Amazon

24242825R00189